'If I'd known who you were...

If I'd been around at the interview...I'd have made sure you didn't get the job.'

Aware that he was no longer jesting, she repeated, 'What are you talking about?'

'You, Dr Marshall, are the last person I would have wanted to join this practice. Even on a temporary basis.'

She was stunned by what she heard. 'Are you saying I'm no good?'

'Far from it,' he replied. 'You are an excellent doctor. And why wouldn't you be? You are your father's daughter. But one Dr Marshall trying to ruin my career is plenty to last a lifetime.'

Barbara Hart was born in Lancashire and educated at a convent in Wales. At twenty-one she moved to New York, where she worked as an advertising copywriter. After two years in the USA she returned to England, where she became a television press officer in charge of publicising a top soap opera and a leading current affairs programme. She gave up her job to write novels. She lives in Cheshire and is married to a solicitor. They have two grown-up sons.

HER FATHER'S DAUGHTER

BY

BARBARA HART

MILLS & BOON

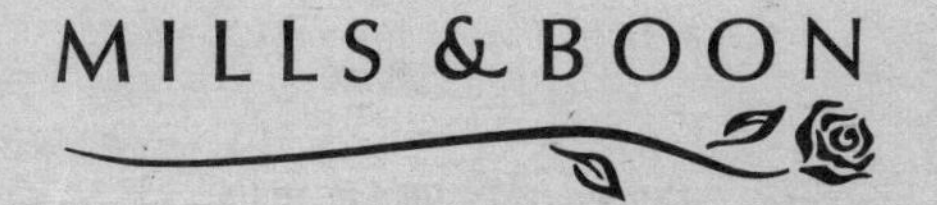

To Roger and Judy.
And with grateful thanks to Helen Sutherland and Maggie Drake, the best of medical advisors.

First published in Great Britain 2000
Harlequin Mills & Boon Limited,
Eton House, 18-24 Paradise Road, Richmond, Surrey TW9 1SR

ISBN 0 263 82233 8

Set in Times Roman 10½ on 12¼ pt.
03-0005-46069

Printed and bound in Spain
by Litografia Rosés, S.A., Barcelona

CHAPTER ONE

KATE MARSHALL felt a tingle of excitement in the pit of her stomach as she drove into the surgery car park in the small Lake District town. The late afternoon sun bathed the tall Lakeland stone building in an amber glow, creating a picture which could have graced the cover of any country living magazine.

To Kate the tingle in her stomach had more to do with what lay inside the building than the picturesque scene outside. This was the culmination of all those years of hard work, study and medical training—her first job in general practice as a qualified doctor.

It was only a temporary position, a six-month contract filling in while one of the doctors in the three-partner group practice took maternity leave, but to Kate it was the fulfilment of a dream. For as long as she could remember she had wanted to work in medicine.

She turned off the engine and, stepping out of her red hatchback, surveyed the scene that greeted her. Exhilaration filled her whole body as she took in the dramatic scenery—mountain ranges stretching out as far as the eye could see, craggy peaks dark against a clear blue sky, fellside streams and grassy slopes, the shimmering waters of the lake.

This must be the medical practice with the best views in the country. She sighed contentedly, strands of blonde hair blowing wildly across her face. She shivered involuntarily as the cool mountain breeze wrapped itself round the thin material of her white silk shirt. Spinning round, she headed towards the large detached house that would be home and workplace for the next six months.

'I'm Dr Kate Marshall,' she told the young woman on the reception desk. 'Dr Morgan is expecting me. Perhaps you'd tell her I've arrived.'

Before the receptionist could make any reply, a tall, broad-shouldered man, who seemed to have appeared from nowhere, rushed up to the reception desk.

'Tracy, would you hand me that spare battery for the mobile phone, please?' he asked pleasantly but firmly. 'It's in the second drawer down.'

Kate found herself jostled out of the way as the man, dressed in mountain gear complete with protective helmet, leaned over the desk. One long-fingered, suntanned hand firmly held a small mobile phone while the other gestured in Tracy's direction.

'As quickly as you can, please,' he said in deep, assertive tones.

Tracy located the spare battery with admirable efficiency and handed it to the man, who seemed in one heck of a hurry. Kate stood back and watched him as he took the battery and fitted it into the phone with strong, capable hands. His expression was intense, the lips of his generous mouth compressed in concentration, his grey eyes the colour of pewter.

Who on earth could he be? mused Kate. Definitely not a doctor, kitted out in all that mountain gear. And surely a patient wouldn't behave like that? A relative of the receptionist's—a brother perhaps? That made the most sense. Whoever he was, he was certainly good-looking.

As the battery clipped into place the man pocketed the mobile phone and bent down to pick up his rucksack. As he did so his eyes fastened on Kate's bare feet in minimal leather sandals, moving upwards along her shapely tanned legs which disappeared into a skimpy denim skirt many inches above her knees.

Standing up again, his powerful frame towered over Kate, whom he seemed to have noticed for the first time. He gave her a look which was a blend of blatant curiosity and sexual interest.

'Sorry for barging in,' he said, 'but this is an emergency.'

'Think nothing of it,' said Kate, a hint of sarcasm creeping into her voice.

He smiled, a warm, easy smile, and despite herself she felt her legs go weak. Then he was gone. Moments later the sound of a car was heard, racing away from the car park.

'Right, where were we?' said Tracy, who seemed not the least put out by being ordered about by a hillwalker in front of strangers. 'Oh, yes, you're waiting to see Dr Morgan. I'll just ring through.' Moments later a smiling, heavily pregnant Dr Jenny Morgan walked into the reception area and greeted Kate.

'Am I glad to see you!' exclaimed Jenny, sticking out her bump in exaggerated fashion, patting it gently. 'You haven't come a moment too soon. I can't wait to stop work and get my feet up for the last month of the pregnancy.'

'I'm really looking forward to starting,' said Kate

with enthusiasm. 'I can begin straight away if that's what you'd like. Is there an evening clinic?'

'Not for me, thank goodness,' replied Jenny. 'It's one of the other partners' surgeries. Technically it should be David's but he's been called out by the mountain rescue team so Gordon will be doing it if he's not back in time. Anyway, Kate, come into my room and we'll chat about things, then I can show you round.'

Kate followed Jenny's rotund figure as she walked, or more accurately waddled, into her consulting room.

'Is David the man I saw a moment ago?' enquired Kate. 'A tall man dressed in mountain gear?'

'Yes,' answered Jenny. 'He's the third partner, the one you didn't meet when you came up for the interview last month. The other partner, Gordon, you did meet. He's out doing his calls at the moment.'

Gordon Sutherland, Kate recalled, was the senior partner in the practice, a pleasant man in his early fifties.

'Can I help out?' offered Kate. 'I really did mean it when I said I was all set to start right away.'

'Wouldn't hear of it,' said Jenny, easing herself into a swivel armchair. 'Anyway, we're not too desperately busy at the moment, thank goodness. No epidemics filling the waiting rooms.'

Kate sat in the patient's chair at the other side of the modern desk and looked around the room that was going to be her office for the next half-year. When she had been up some weeks ago she had been interviewed in Gordon's room, which was very similar in size and decor to this one. The walls and carpet were in warm pastel tones of pale apricot and honey. Modern office furniture with smooth rounded lines, also in pastel colours, contrasted with the clinical white of the washbasin and sterile equipment area. A simple vase of freshly cut flowers stood on a ledge next to the window, which had a magnificent view of the mountains.

'That other partner,' ventured Kate, 'the one in the mountaineering gear—is he often...up mountains?' For some reason she found herself fascinated by the man with the steely grey eyes and the deep brown voice.

'David? Well, he's called out from time to time on mountain rescue,' explained Jenny. 'It's voluntary, of course, but we all feel it's a very worthwhile and vital service, particularly living up here. We cover for him whenever necessary. David is ideally suited to being the team's medic as he's a keen hill-walker himself. I'm glad to say it's Gordon's turn tonight, not mine, to cover for him. Anyway, we can't throw you in at the deep end the moment you walk through the door. We'll wait till tomorrow to do that!'

After taking Kate round the ground floor of the house, showing her the other partners' consulting rooms, pointing out the kitchen and coffee-machine area and the doctors' sitting room area behind Reception, Jenny officially introduced Kate to Tracy the receptionist.

'There's also Trish whom you'll meet this evening. She does the evening clinics and shares the secretarial duties with Tracy,' Jenny explained. 'I'm just going to show Dr Marshall her flat,' said Jenny to Tracy. 'That's where I'll be if you need me.'

Kate followed Jenny up the stairs.

'You timed your arrival perfectly,' said Jenny over her shoulder. 'In between clinics. The only patients we'll have for the next hour or so will be those coming in to pick up prescriptions. So, barring emergencies, we can make a cup of tea in your flat and continue our chat.'

The flat on the first floor of the house was small but perfectly adequate for Kate's needs. It was freshly painted and decorated and smelled of new carpets.

'It all looks very nice,' said Kate, walking into the neat bedroom which had matching Laura Ashley curtains and bedlinen.

'You should have seen it before!' replied Jenny, sitting down on the edge of the bed. 'This is the first time we've had a live-in locum so it's all spanking new. David's flat is on the floor above. He's been living over the shop since he joined the partnership three years ago. It seemed an ideal arrangement at the time. It was good from a security point of view to have someone living on the premises, and with David being single it suited him as well. He said it would save him from having to look for a flat or a house in the town.'

'It could have its drawbacks, I suppose, living "over the shop", as you put it,' reflected Kate.

'You mean always being available, particularly in the middle of the night? You needn't worry,' replied Jenny. 'We sorted that out ages ago. Our practice is in a night rota system with other doctors in two nearby towns. Each doctor only has to be on night call once every two weeks.' Jenny began to ease herself off the bed. 'I'll show you the kitchen and then we can make that cup of tea. Ouch!'

A spasm of pain crossed Jenny's face and she clutched her stomach.

Kate, who had been admiring the view of the mountains and lake from the bedroom window, turned quickly to look at Jenny. 'Are you all right?' she asked with concern.

Jenny breathed out slowly. 'Yes,' she said shakily. 'It's just a little gastric pain I've been having on and off all day.'

'When you say gastric pain,' said Kate with deliberation, 'do you mean contraction?'

Jenny levered herself off the bed. 'I'm not sure. The trouble is, this is my first baby and I don't know what a contraction feels like. It's all very well, me telling other expectant mothers about childbirth, but unless you've actually gone through labour yourself you don't really know what it's going to feel like. So it could be contractions I've been having all day, or it could be a gastric infection.'

She heaved her bulk out of the bedroom and into the small kitchen fitted with limed oak units. A 'welcome' bag of groceries was on the kitchen table and inside the fridge was fresh orange juice, milk and a bottle of wine.

'That's so thoughtful of you,' said Kate gratefully, going over to the sink and filling the kettle with water. 'Tea or coffee?'

Jenny did not reply immediately and Kate continued to fill the kettle from the tap. When she turned round she saw Jenny bent double, clutching her stomach and holding her breath. Putting the kettle down with a crash, Kate rushed over to her.

'Jenny, I think you'd better come and lie down on the bed for a few minutes. You're obviously not well.'

After a few seconds the pain left Jenny's face and she gave Kate a glance filled with apprehension. But when she spoke her voice was calm. 'I think my labour's started. The pains are pretty regular. Would you ask Tracy to phone for an ambulance, please?'

Kate helped her up from the kitchen chair. 'First of all I'm going to get you lying down on the bed and then—'

Before she could finish the sentence, Jenny gave a sharp intake of breath. 'Oh,' she gasped almost in disbelief, 'my waters have broken! All systems go, I think...'

'I'd better examine you, Jenny, and see how far things have progressed,' said Kate briskly.

Kate helped her onto the bed and went to wash her hands in the bathroom, before returning to give Jenny an internal examination. What she discovered made her heart race.

'Your cervix is almost fully dilated. The head's well down. I think you're going to deliver quite soon. How many weeks are you?'

'Thirty-six,' gasped Jenny between contractions.

'I'll get Tracy to call for that ambulance,' said Kate, 'but I'll pick up my medical bag from the car just in case. I'm sure you'll make it to the hospital, Jenny. First babies always take ages.'

She ran out, calling behind her, 'Just keep doing the breathing exercises. I'll be back in no time.'

Two minutes later, as Kate ran back into her flat, she heard Jenny calling out.

'Quick, Kate,' she said with a note of panic in her voice. 'I think I'm into the second stage of labour already. I'm sure the baby's coming. I've got this irresistible urge to *push!*' Saying the last word loudly, she lay back on the bed and starting panting in short, quick breaths.

Dropping her medical bag at the foot of the bed, Kate rushed into the bathroom. She thoroughly washed her hands and arms up to the elbows, then, grabbing armfuls of the new fluffy white towels from the airing cupboard, turned to go back to Jenny. As an afterthought Kate pulled down the brand new plastic shower curtain to use as a mattress protector.

She slipped the plastic curtain and a couple of the towels under Jenny's back, then pulled on a pair of latex gloves. She took another look to see how labour was progressing and listened with her stethoscope to the foetal heartbeat.

'You're doing fine, both of you,' she said reassuringly to Jenny. 'I'd say you were fully dilated. No wonder you want to push. Here comes another contraction. Now push!'

Kate was helping Jenny to hold up her legs and propped up her back as she bore down. With one big push the head was delivered. As Kate eased out the baby's shoulders she told Jenny to pant and hold back for a moment. Then, on Kate's instructions, Jenny gave one final push and her baby slithered into the world.

After completing the usual procedures, Kate cleared the mucus from the air passages and listened to the baby's chest through her stethoscope. She flicked the soles of the tiny feet with her fingers and in that instant the baby drew up her legs and gave a shuddering breath. 'A lovely, healthy little girl,' said Kate as she laid the baby gently on Jenny's breast. 'She's small, but her lungs are perfectly fit.' And just to prove it the tiny creature let out a bellow of rage.

'I think I'll have all my babies prematurely if they're as quick and easy as that,' said Jenny.

By the time the ambulance arrived Jenny was sitting up, holding her new baby wrapped in a pristine white towel. Kate had delivered babies before, but never in such dramatic circumstances and never alone. She felt a glow of pride as she handed Jenny and the new baby over to the paramedics who would now take them to the hospital.

There was a pounding of boots on the stairs and David's dishevelled figure appeared in the doorway just as the ambulance crew were stretchering Jenny out of the bedroom. He was bare-headed and in his shirtsleeves, still wearing walking trousers and boots.

'What's going on here?' he asked with concern, pushing past Kate into the room.

'Nothing to worry about. I've just had a baby!' said Jenny, a glow of pride and achievement spreading across her pale face.

'Good grief,' exclaimed David. 'Is everything all right? Hadn't I better call the prem unit and warn them?' He looked with concern at the small bundle wrapped in Kate's towel, now being carried by one of the paramedics.

'I already did that,' replied Kate, 'but it's probably unnecessary. The baby seems fine and she's only a little smaller than a full-term baby.'

'And how would you know?' He rounded on her, his gaze taking in her flimsy blouse and miniskirt. 'I hardly think you're in a position to give a medical opinion.'

'Well, I...' spluttered Kate, taken aback by his manner.

'You *are* a patient, I take it,' he said in a calmer tone of voice. 'I saw you in Reception before I left on the mountain rescue.'

Then, ignoring Kate, he turned back to the paramedics. 'I really think I should examine the baby before you take her in the ambulance. She may need to be put straight in an incubator.'

'I *told* you,' interrupted Kate, 'I have already examined her and deemed it safe for her to travel to the hospital as she is. Don't worry,' she assured the paramedics, 'I shall take full responsibility.'

'And who on earth are *you* to take full responsibility?' He eyed her with hostility and impatience.

She reddened. 'I'm a doctor,' she snapped. 'Your new locum.'

Jenny's stretcher drew level with them. 'Let me introduce you two. David, this is Dr Kate Marshall. Kate, this is Dr David Firth. Now we really must be off.'

David's mouth fell open in embarrassment. 'I'm most awfully sorry, Dr Marshall,' he apologised with genuine remorse at his gaffe. 'It's just that when I saw you in Reception I presumed—'

'Don't worry, Dr Firth,' replied Kate. 'When I saw you in Reception you didn't strike me as being a doctor either!'

They saw Jenny and the baby safely into the ambulance and walked back to Kate's flat. At the door she turned to face David. With all the anxiety and drama of the birth Kate hadn't taken in the details of David's features, but something about his voice had seemed familiar to her.

He was no longer wearing his helmet and for the first time she was able to study his face. His dark, almost black, tousled hair fell forward over his brow. His chiselled face was smudged with mud. But that wasn't what made Kate stare so intensely at him.

'What's the matter?' he asked. 'Seen a ghost?'

'Yes, I think so,' replied Kate.

He was broader and more muscular than she remembered him, but it *had* been twelve years ago. His lean frame had now consolidated and matured, but he still had that same brooding, sensual look, those dark, penetrating eyes. And he was still the most handsome man she had ever known.

'David Firth.' She said the words to herself. 'How could I forget?'

His brow furrowed questioningly. He was searching the recesses of his mind.

'I'm Kate Marshall,' she said. 'My father is Dr Ewan Marshall. You were one of his best medical students. You were twenty-one. I was only a kid of fifteen so you probably don't remember me. But I remember you. You used to spend a lot of time at our house. In fact, you were the main reason I became a doctor. I had a terrible crush on you.'

Terrible crush? She smiled wryly to herself. She'd been besotted by the handsome young student as only a teenager could have been, her every waking thought filled with images of David Firth.

All the time she had been speaking, David had been scrutinising her. As recognition dawned, an unreadable look came over his face and he stood stock-still, like a statue. Then, as if blinking away some unwelcome memory, he allowed a slow smile to spread over his face.

'Katie Marshall,' he murmured softly. 'Little Katie Marshall. Of course I remember you!'

He stepped closer. Putting his hands on her hair, he pulled it gently back from her face into a ponytail, the way she had once worn it.

'Yes. Now I see it. The same natural blonde hair.' He let it fall back onto her shoulders as his strong fingers traced a line round her face. This was a girl he had looked on as a young sister, the sister he'd never had. But with a jolt he knew he was now looking at her in quite a different way…as a man looked at a desirable woman. He spoke his thoughts out loud. 'That tomboy face has become so…beautiful.'

To her embarrassment she found she was blushing at his compliment. 'Oh, stop it, you old smoothie,' she teased.

'No, I mean it. I'm not a flatterer, Kate, believe me. It's quite a shock, finding you here, walking into my life again.'

'It's quite a shock for me, too,' responded Kate.

'For a start I never expected to find you working as a GP. Weren't you planning a hospital career?'

'That's right,' confirmed David. 'I qualified as an anaesthetist. But I decided that conscious patients were more interesting than unconscious ones so I switched to general practice.'

His eyes were taking in every detail of her. It was an examination that made Kate feel more like a patient than a colleague. 'So what about you?' he enquired.

'I'd always wanted to be what I used to call a "real" doctor,' explained Kate. 'I'm afraid I never considered Dad to be a proper doctor, even though, of course, he was. To me he was just an academic—a teacher. And when I was a little girl the doctors-and-nurses outfits represented the real thing to me. As far as I was concerned, a real doctor had a stethoscope round his neck and a big Gladstone bag filled with bottles of pills.'

'Whereas your father just had stacks of boring old books from floor to ceiling!' said David with a laugh. 'Not a toy stethoscope in sight.'

Kate could feel a warmth developing between them, an easy banter.

'I'm ashamed to say I would never have recognised you,' he said guiltily. 'But that's not to say I don't remember you. I certainly do. You were a delightful young girl. Full of fun and optimism. And your teenage crush did my morale a world of good. So how about a hug for old times?'

Suddenly the masculine strength of his arms were around her slender body. The thrilling scent of him made her senses reel. He radiated a heat that seared right through her.

It was a brotherly hug on his part, Kate surmised. He was no doubt recalling the fifteen-year-old, waif-like creature who used to follow him round adoringly all those years ago. The big brother she'd never had. The dedicated young man who had so impressed her with his love of medicine that she'd vowed to follow in his footsteps.

As he hugged her in a warm, lingering embrace he was probably taking a trip down memory lane, concluded Kate. He would be recalling how her father, top medical academic Dr Ewan Marshall, had treated him like a son. He'd always said David had been the most promising of his medical students and had taken the young man under his wing.

David's own father was an army doctor and he and his family had been posted overseas. As a result David had seen little of them during his university days. Kate's father and stepmother, Julia, had given an open invitation to David who, for the best part of a year, had seemed to spend all his free time as one of their family. There had even been talk of him moving into the self-contained flat at the top of their rambling Victorian house.

But it had all ended abruptly. David had stopped coming to the house and Kate's parents had never mentioned him again.

Releasing her from his bear-like hug, David stepped back and looked at her. Kate thought it was her imagination, but his expression was beginning to change before her eyes. He now had the mouth of a man holding back some strong emotion.

'Why did you stop coming to our house?' asked Kate. 'No one ever told me.'

David turned away and she was unable to read the look on his face as he said casually, 'I moved to a different medical school.'

He strode quickly to the stairs leading to the floor above. 'Now I must shower before evening clinic,' he said, disappearing up the stairs to his own flat.

It was like a dream. One moment he was there, the next he was gone. It was as if David Firth had never come back into her life. Kate might have believed she'd imagined it all had it not been for the fact that for several minutes afterwards she could still feel the warm glow of his body on hers.

Up in his own flat, David stripped off his muddy clothes and stepped into the all-embracing warmth of the shower. It was a moment he anticipated with relish after a mountain rescue, but today the enjoyment of the hot water beating on his aching muscles gave him no pleasure. His mind was elsewhere. He, too, could still feel the warmth of Kate's body on his. What a fool he had been to give her that impetuous hug! Keep away from her, David Firth, warned a small inner voice.

'Keep away,' he said out loud as the water, pounding against his chest and arms, refused to wash away the seductive sensation of holding that particular woman in his embrace.

CHAPTER TWO

'AND so it's probably a good idea if Kate sits in with one of us for the first day or so to ease her into the practice gently.'

It was early next morning and Gordon Sutherland was chairing a practice meeting in his consulting room. Jenny's abrupt departure had upset their arrangements. The partners had originally intended that Kate would sit in with Jenny for a few days, familiarising herself with the practice routine before taking over Jenny's patients.

'As you've got the morning clinic, David, I suggest Kate starts there. She can come out with me on house calls this afternoon.'

It sounded an eminently sensible idea to Kate but David didn't appear over-enthusiastic.

'Kate may not like the idea of sitting in on my patients,' said David evasively. 'After all, she's fully qualified and quite capable of running her own clinics and looking after her own patients.'

Gordon looked puzzled. 'That's not the point, is it?' he replied. 'This is a group practice so it doesn't matter who sees the patients. And running a country practice like ours is quite different from the large medical-centre type practices Kate has been used to in her training. Our local hospital, for instance, is tiny compared with what she has been used to. And going out on home visits in the wilds of Cumbria can be a bit daunting for someone who doesn't know the area.'

David said nothing. Gordon pressed on. 'We discussed all this weeks ago and agreed this was a friendlier way for our new locum to be introduced into the practice. I'm sure Kate sees it that way. Jenny and I mentioned it at your interview, didn't we, Kate?'

'I would certainly be happier shadowing you both for a couple of days,' confirmed Kate. 'I'm perfectly confident dealing with medical matters, but I think I'd get to know the practice better and quicker doing it the way Gordon suggests.'

'Right then, that's settled,' said David, his face an unreadable mask.

'Would you ask Mrs Hughes to come in, please, Tracy?' David said into the desk intercom.

Mrs Hughes would be the fourth patient this morning. So far they'd seen a forestry worker with an infected finger, a man needing a medical for an insurance firm and a baby for an inoculation jab.

Kate had been impressed by the care and interest David had shown to each patient, asking the necessary questions with the minimum of fuss, examining them gently yet thoroughly, and handing out prescriptions, jabs and signed forms with workmanlike efficiency.

To the patients he must seem like a model GP, she concluded. But whenever they were alone in the room David's attitude changed. Kate got the distinct feeling that David wasn't at all happy having her sitting in on his clinic. In fact, she'd put it stronger than that...he hated having her there.

What on earth was the matter with the man? He had never previously struck her as the moody kind, yet today that was exactly how she would have described him.

Kate kept her thoughts to herself. The next patient, Mrs Hughes, came in. She was an attractive brown-haired woman in her late thirties. David had handed her notes to Kate earlier for her to read up on the case. Mrs Hughes had been trying unsuccessfully for a long time to become pregnant. She and her husband had spent many years and thousands of pounds on a variety of fertility treatments.

'Sit down, Mrs Hughes,' said David. 'You don't mind if my colleague, Dr Marshall, sits in on this consultation, do you? She's going to be working in the practice for the next few months, temporarily replacing Dr Morgan who, by the way, had a baby yesterday. A little girl.'

Kate thought this was a rather tactless thing to say to a woman who was desperately trying to have a baby herself. Rubbing her nose in it, you might say. But then all became clear as David waved a piece of paper at Mrs Hughes.

'Speaking of which,' he said, smiling at her, 'the results of your test have come back from the lab. They're positive. No doubt about it this time. Congratulations, Mrs Hughes, you're pregnant.'

Kate had often read the words 'her face lit up', but until that moment she had never appreciated the full meaning of the words. The woman sitting opposite them was positively incandescent with delight.

'Oh, that's fantastic!' she gasped. 'Are you really sure, Doctor? There can't be any mistake, like last time?' A troubled look clouded her face as if she thought this treasure might be snatched from her grasp.

'No doubt at all,' confirmed David. 'Last time, if you remember, you used one of those do-it-yourself kits from the chemist, which can sometimes give false results.'

David looked at her notes. 'It's early days, of course. According to the date of your last period, you should now be six weeks pregnant.'

The two doctors looked at Mrs Hughes as she took in this momentous news.

'Six weeks pregnant,' she said incredulously. Looking down at her completely flat stomach, she patted it gently. 'I'd better start buying some maternity clothes!'

David and Kate laughed along with her. It was a lovely shared experience, a real 'feel good' moment. The kind of moment that made it all worthwhile.

As he walked with her to the door, having checked her weight and blood pressure, David said, 'You may get a little morning sickness for the next few weeks, but that's nothing to worry about. I've put a note on your file for Tracy to make an initial hospital appointment for you, but after that you can come to us for your routine antenatal checks if that suits you better.'

'Yes, I would prefer to come to you,' said Mrs Hughes, still barely able to believe that finally, after all the years of disappointment, she was going to have a baby.

'Eat a healthy diet, take regular exercise—nothing strenuous, of course—and come back in six weeks' time.'

Taking a coffee-break together, David seemed to lighten up a little. The pleasure he had derived from giving Mrs Hughes her good news had lifted his spirits and put him in a much better mood towards Kate.

Even so, Kate needed to say something.

'David, if you don't want me sitting in on your clinic, just say so,' she said, trying to keep her voice matter-of-fact.

'I don't mind in the least,' he said, pouring himself a coffee from the filter machine, deliberately avoiding eye contact.

That afternoon, Kate accompanied Gordon on his rounds. They seemed to drive for miles between each house call through narrow country lanes and over steep mountain passes.

'Now you can see why we didn't think it a good idea to leave you to your fate around these parts,' said Gordon on the way to one particularly remote farmhouse.

'I'm very glad you didn't,' said Kate. 'It would look pretty feeble if the doctor on call got lost. Orienteering isn't one of the subjects they teach at medical school!'

'How are you settling in?' asked Gordon, manoeuvring his way round a group of sheep that had wandered across the road. 'You had a rather dramatic introduction to the practice, delivering a baby before you'd had time to take your hat and coat off, metaphorically speaking! Apart from that, how are things going? Is the flat all right?'

'It's wonderful,' replied Kate. 'Much nicer than anything I've had before.' She wondered whether she should mention David's odd behaviour to Gordon. Or would that seem like telling tales? Especially as Gordon was David's senior partner.

She decided to hold her tongue and hope things got better. Maybe the abrupt change of mood and the way he'd left her flat last night could be put down to exhaustion after the exertion of the mountain rescue. But this morning, what had all that been about? Six months of unfriendly behaviour like that was something she was definitely not looking forward to.

The following day would have been Jenny's morning clinic had she still been around to take it. Gordon had been called out to one of his cardiac patients and so the clinic fell to David once again. And once again Kate sat in with him.

Any hopes she'd had that his cool behaviour towards her had been a temporary phase were dashed when he continued to treat her with a distant, polite courtesy throughout the morning. When she recalled the warmth of his welcoming embrace only two days before she found the dramatic change in his attitude both mysterious and hurtful.

She resolved that she must speak diplomatically about it to Gordon later that day when she would be sitting in on one of his clinics. Maybe he could throw some light on it. The bad atmosphere was beginning to affect her more than she could have believed possible. If she was to make a success of working in the group practice, she had to clear the air between them.

When she did broach the subject with Gordon shortly after lunch, he was taken aback. 'Are you sure?' he asked. 'David? Unfriendly? I find that very hard to believe. I would expect David to do everything he could to make you feel welcome. He's that kind of man.'

Kate felt uncomfortable, discussing a colleague in this way, but she knew she had to get things out in the open.

'Believe me, Gordon, I'm most unhappy talking about David behind his back like this, but I just don't know who else I can talk to about it.' Kate looked very downcast. 'You see, it's beginning to affect how I feel about working here.'

'Then you were quite right to come and see me, Kate,' said Gordon. 'Anything that intrudes on the smooth running of the practice in the long term affects our patients and the service we give them. They are our top priority, and personality clashes between the doctors must be avoided at all costs. Leave it to me to sort out.'

Kate felt happier already. Having unburdened herself to this kindly, sympathetic man, she felt things would now start to look up.

At the end of the afternoon clinic Gordon chatted for a while with Kate about some of the patients they had just seen, their medical backgrounds and family members who were also patients of the practice. Kate was beginning at last to feel part of the team and less of an outsider.

'Would you like to come to supper tonight?' asked

Gordon as she was leaving his room. 'Jean wants to meet you and tonight is as good a night as any. By the way, Jean's a district nurse–midwife, so we can have a good old medical gossip. I'll invite David along, too. A social occasion might help smooth things out between you two.'

An hour later, Kate had just poured herself a coffee in the small kitchen area and was taking it back to her room. As she passed by Gordon's room the door was slightly ajar and she could hear the voices of Gordon and David.

Eavesdropping on private conversations wasn't something Kate made a habit of doing, but on this occasion she felt she had a vested interest, especially as she heard her own name mentioned.

Walking back to her room as slowly as she thought reasonable, she picked up snatches of sentences.

Gordon's distinct Scottish tones carried through the small gap. 'Yes, I understand what you're saying, David, but you should make an effort to be nice to her.'

David's reply was harder to make out. Gordon spoke again.

'Well, it won't kill you to be friendly to her. After all it's only for six months. And you know what they say about the sins of the fathers not being visited on the children.'

Kate walked into her room, and only just in time for David must have left Gordon's room and was now entering his own room, shutting the door behind him.

She placed her cup on the desk and sat down

heavily in her chair. They said eavesdroppers never learned anything good about themselves, thought Kate ruefully. But she hadn't actually learned anything at all, good or bad. Just something extremely puzzling.

What on earth had they been talking about? And how could a Biblical quotation about 'the sins of the fathers' have any relevance to her, or to David for that matter? Kate was now in a thorough state of confusion.

As she was pondering the issue, David popped his head round her door. He was smiling at her for the first time in two days. Gordon's talk had evidently had some effect.

'Hi,' he said, stepping into the room. He looked the epitome of the country doctor in a beautifully cut tweed jacket. A warm smile spread across his tanned face. Kate felt a stab of sexual awareness dart through her. She collected her thoughts, irritated by how easily this man could manipulate her feelings.

'I believe we're both supper guests at the Sutherlands tonight,' he said. His body language and facial expression exuded friendliness and charm. The magic words Gordon had said to him had obviously done the trick.

'That's right,' she said, returning his friendly smile, 'but I forgot to ask him where they live.'

'Not to worry,' he said lightly. 'We'll go together. I suggest we leave here about seven-thirty, OK?'

'OK,' replied Kate, who now felt a childlike happiness spreading through her body. And all because some man had given her a friendly smile!

But it wasn't just any man, was it? she reflected.

It was David Firth, the man she'd lost her heart to when she'd been a foolish fifteen-year-old, the man who could still tug at her heartstrings even now when she was supposed to be a sensible twenty-seven-year-old.

Oh, grow up, Kate! she said sharply to herself.

Her hands were shaking as she began to get ready that evening. She had picked out her dress before taking her shower—black, sleeveless and figure-hugging with a short skirt that left her long legs bare.

Her freshly washed hair shone with summer highlights. Her make-up was lightly applied to her flawless skin. But the dress? She had forgotten just how tight and how short it was. Doubts crept into her mind. Was it suitable for an informal supper at a colleague's house? She reached for her cream linen jacket and slipped it over her shoulders. It made all the difference, toning down the sensuality of the dress as the jacket sleeves covered her bare arms.

Moments later she heard a door open and shut, then footsteps coming down the stairs. Even if she'd wanted to change her mind it was now too late.

Kate opened the door to his knock. 'Your chauffeur awaits.' His face was serious but his eyes were laughing. He was casually dressed in freshly laundered jeans and a crisp pale blue shirt with thin white stripes. He looked wonderful.

As she moved closer to him on her way out of the flat, the tangy scent of his soap mingled with the subtle hint of her perfume. His eyes held a look of desire as he took in her outfit. He said nothing. But his scrutiny made a pulse beat hard in her throat.

* * *

Gordon and Jean lived about a mile away in a beautifully restored Lakeland stone cottage.

Jean greeted them warmly. 'You must be Kate,' she said. 'It's lovely to meet you.' David followed her inside and kissed Jean on the cheek.

At supper David was a model of gentlemanly behaviour, attentive, amusing and charming. It was all too good to be true. Kate was uneasy. Her instinct told her he was putting on an act for her benefit. Only once did he let his charming mask slip.

Jean was handing a coffee-cup to Kate and asked, 'Is anyone else in your family in medicine?'

'My father is a doctor,' replied Kate. 'He used to teach David at medical school.'

'Oh, how interesting,' she said. 'Did you know that, Gordon?'

Kate was aware of an immediate drop in temperature.

Gordon spoke sharply. 'I did tell you, Jean, actually.' He fixed her with a don't-say-any-more look.

Kate looked across at David who wouldn't meet her gaze. His face was grim, his mouth tense.

'Are we likely to get an increase in our funding next year, do you think?' said Gordon, hastily changing the subject.

Before David could answer, his mobile phone rang. Taking it from his shirt pocket, he extended the aerial. 'David Firth,' he said, speaking into the mouthpiece.

Conversation came to a halt while David took his call.

'When was that?' he asked calmly. A pause. 'Right. I'll be along straight away. Just give me a note of your address.' David scribbled an address on a scrap of paper handed to him by Jean. He ended the call and pulled down the aerial.

'That was Mr Hughes,' he told them all. 'His wife's pregnant and she's got stomach pains. She's also had slight bleeding.'

'Mrs Hughes. Isn't she the woman who's been trying for years to have a baby?' recalled Kate.

'I'm afraid so. It may be nothing to worry about, but because of her history of fertility treatment I feel I must go round and see her.' David rose from his chair. 'I'm sorry to break up the evening. Would you give Kate a lift home, Gordon? I don't know how long I'll be at the Hughes'.'

'Mind if I come, too?' asked Kate. 'After all, I was with you at the clinic yesterday when you confirmed her pregnancy. I feel I have an interest in what happens in this particular case.'

'Be my guest,' said David as he walked with her to the door.

When they saw Mrs Hughes ten minutes later, she was grey with pain, lying curled up on the settee.

David took her temperature and blood pressure and then with gentle hands examined her abdomen. 'Is that where it hurts?' he asked.

'Yes,' she replied quietly, unable to hide the fear in her voice.

'How much blood have you lost?'

'Not much. Only a little bit.'

David stood back and put his hand on Kate's arm. 'I'd like Dr Marshall to look at you, if that's all right, Mrs Hughes.' David locked eyes with Kate. His look said it all. It was bad news.

Kate moved her hands softly round the patient's stomach. The uterus felt enlarged.

'You're six weeks pregnant, aren't you, Mrs Hughes?' said Kate, mentally trying to visualise how large the uterus should normally be by six weeks. She pulled down her stethoscope and turned to David, murmuring under her breath, 'Possible ectopic.'

David's eyes met hers in confirmation.

'Mrs Hughes,' he said gently, 'I think I'd like you in hospital for some checks.'

As he spoke, a spasm of pain caused her to bend double.

Her husband looked on anxiously. 'Isn't there anything you can give her now, Doctor, to stop the pain?'

'I'm reluctant to give her anything until we get her into hospital, Mr Hughes. Just in case we have to operate.'

'Oh, my God,' he said in shock.

'How long since you had anything to eat?' David asked Mrs Hughes. 'Did you have an evening meal?'

'No,' she replied weakly. 'I haven't felt like eating all day.'

'That's good,' said David, pulling up his mobile aerial and dialling. 'In that case we could operate straight away if necessary.' He spoke into the mobile phone. 'This is Dr Firth. Put me through to Dr Evans, the gynaecologist, please.'

There was a short pause while the call was being put through. David put his hand over the mouthpiece and said to Kate, 'Call an ambulance, will you, Kate? Use their phone. That'll speed things up.

'John, it's David Firth here. We have a suspected ectopic pregnancy. A Mrs Sophie Hughes. I'm sending her round in a blue-light ambulance.' He was about to end the call when something the gynaecologist said made him pause. 'That's no problem,' he replied. 'I'm an anaesthetist. I can even provide you with another doctor to assist in Theatre. See you in fifteen minutes.'

The impact of the phone call had hit home. Mrs Hughes burst into tears. 'Ectopic pregnancy? Does that mean I'll lose the baby?'

'No, Sophie, no,' said her husband, comforting her.

'If it is ectopic, I'm afraid it does mean losing the baby, Mrs Hughes.' David imparted this information as gently as possible. Even so, it had a catastrophic effect on both Mr and Mrs Hughes.

'No!' they cried in unison.

'Look, Doctor, my wife's gone through years of treatment and tests and raised hopes to get this far,' said the distraught husband. 'Don't tell us now we could lose the baby. Can't we just hold on and see if the pain goes away? Sophie's brave. She'll put up with anything to keep this baby.'

Mr Hughes's voice was rising to near hysteria. His wife joined in. 'I don't want to go to hospital. You mustn't operate! I won't let you take away my baby! I won't let you!'

'No, we won't let you,' he said, collapsing on the settee next to her.

Kate was appalled. It was a nightmare scenario. Would they now have to drag this poor woman into the ambulance, beating off an attack from her husband?

David pulled the frenzied Mr Hughes to his feet. Taking him to one side, he spoke with icy coolness. 'You are risking your wife's life, Mr Hughes. Just calm down, and think rationally.

'If your baby is growing in the wrong place—in a Fallopian tube, for instance—it isn't going to be viable anyway. It will die. And if we don't remove it quickly the tube will burst, and your wife could also die. Now, for God's sake, try and calm her down, not whip her up into a state of hysteria.'

David's firm words had the desired effect. By the time the ambulance pulled up outside the house, Mr Hughes was giving his wife all the moral support she needed. They both went in the ambulance which set off at speed, siren wailing, blue light flashing, to the hospital.

David and Kate followed in David's four-wheel drive. On the short journey David explained his conversation with the hospital gynaecologist.

'There's another emergency op going on at the moment. The general surgeon's doing it and he's using the anaesthetist on call. John Evans, the gynae, said there may be some delay before he can operate on our patient so I told him I could handle the anaesthetics and that you could assist in Theatre. That way we won't waste vital minutes.'

Adrenalin surged through Kate's veins, making her more alert than she'd been all evening. 'I suppose there's always an outside chance it could be nothing serious,' she said, more in hope than anything else.

'Are you kidding?' he said, racing along in the

wake of the ambulance siren. 'The swollen abdomen, the pelvic pain, the vaginal bleeding. Classic symptoms of a Fallopian pregnancy. Plus the fact she's been on fertility treatment. That makes her four times more likely than other women to have an ectopic.'

Recalling the look of unalloyed joy on Sophie Hughes's face only the day before, Kate felt desperately sad for her. 'Life can be very unfair,' she sighed.

CHAPTER THREE

THE gynaecologist John Evans, Kate and David were in their blue theatre tops and trousers, scrubbing up together. As they put on their theatre garb, David finally got round to introducing John to Kate.

'John, meet my new locum for the next six months and your new theatre assistant for tonight,' he said, pulling on his rubber gloves and walking towards the anaesthetic room. 'Now that we all know each other, I'll start anaesthetising for the laparoscopy.'

A short time later David and the theatre technician wheeled the unconscious Sophie Hughes into the operating theatre. 'I've given her Thiopentone,' said David. 'We can top it up if open surgery goes ahead.'

'Fine,' said John. 'I'll just have a look around with the laparoscope to see what's going on inside.'

Sophie was prepared and towelled up for the initial exploratory operation to find out if Kate and David's diagnosis was correct.

Making a tiny incision in her stomach, John introduced the laparoscope and moved it around the area of Sophie's left Fallopian tube.

'That seems normal,' he said, studying the screen. But as he moved to the right Fallopian tube, it was a different story. A red swelling the size of a large olive was distorting the passageway close to the ovary.

'That's it,' said the surgeon, observing the unwelcome evidence of a misplaced embryo. 'There's the poor little mite who's growing in the wrong place.'

Moving the laparoscope around the area, his voice was grim. 'There's bleeding, too,' he said gravely. 'Looks as if it has already ruptured. I'd like to proceed to open surgery straight away.'

He glanced up at David for confirmation. 'Is that all right with you? Patient sufficiently under?'

'No problem,' confirmed David, checking Sophie's breathing, heartbeat and blood pressure.

With admirable efficiency and expediency the staff nurse and theatre sister removed the laparoscope and wheeled in another trolley with more instruments and towels.

'Ready, Sister,' barked John, who was immediately handed a scalpel from the overhead table. He turned to Kate. 'You'll be retracting, I assume.' It was said as a statement, not a question.

'Yes,' replied Kate as retractor and swabs were put in her hands by the attentive staff nurse.

The initial incision was made, clips and artery forceps holding the wound open for a further, deeper cut into the abdomen. Watery blood spurted out.

Moving with speed and dexterity, John located the site of the ectopic pregnancy and examined it with his fingers.

'We shall have to take the tube and the ovary out, I'm afraid. It's ruptured and it's too much of a mess to leave inside her.' His voice was calm but there was no hiding the gravity of his words.

By now there was a lot of free fluid in the abdomen. Kate and the theatre sister were constantly swabbing and using suction to keep the abdominal cavity as dry as possible.

'Blood pressure's dropping,' said David calmly.

'It's all that bleeding,' said John, making another incision. 'How fast is it dropping?'

'Too fast for comfort,' replied David. 'Can we hurry things up a little, please?'

'I'll apply another artery clamp,' said Kate, feeling panic rising in her throat.

Over his mask David glanced at Kate across the operating table. Their eyes locked, and for a brief moment it was as if they were the only two people in the room as they battled to save the life of Sophie Hughes.

The tension was tangible as the team worked to complete the operation. Kate assisted John to suture the wound. Swabs and instruments were counted, and finally it was all over.

'She looks a good colour,' said David with relief in his voice as Sophie was wheeled into the recovery area.

'Ironic, isn't it?' said John wearily. 'In order to save one life, you have to take another. I'm assuming this was a wanted baby.'

'Very much so,' said David.

'We'd better speak to the husband,' said John, peeling off his gloves. 'This is the bit I hate. Giving the bad news.'

'Don't worry, John,' said David. 'You've done everything you need to do. She's our patient after all. We'll do the dirty work.' He took Kate by the arm and steered her from the operating theatre.

Outside in the corridor sat a grim-faced Mr

Hughes. His eyes held a glimmer of hope as David and Kate came through the swing doors and approached him.

'Your wife is fine, Mr Hughes,' said David, 'but I'm afraid we were unable to save the baby. It was an ectopic pregnancy. The Fallopian tube had ruptured so there was no time to be lost before operating.'

The hope died in Mr Hughes's eyes. 'Well, that's it, I suppose.'

'There's no reason why your wife shouldn't go on to have a perfectly normal pregnancy next time,' assured David. 'No reason at all. And she can at least take comfort from the fact that she now knows she can fall pregnant. She has conceived once, she can do it again.'

Driving home in the early hours, David and Kate were silent. The unspoken relationship which had built up between them in the operating theatre hung like a promise in the air. The shared experience of battling for the life of a patient was not a rarity, given their profession, but each time it happened it was a special moment, a moment that put everything else into perspective.

The car wheels crunched on the car-park gravel.

Switching off the engine, David turned to Kate. 'Fancy a nightcap? It always takes me a good half-hour to wind down after a call-out like that.'

'Good idea,' replied Kate. 'Your place or mine? I can offer tea, coffee or cocoa.'

'I can offer brandy.'

'Your place wins.' Kate slid her long legs out of the Range Rover.

David's flat was similar in size to hers, but it had a more lived-in feel about it. Kate followed him into the kitchen. It was fitted with pine units with a pine table in the centre. The white stone sink matched the white paintwork, and the walls were a dark, almost navy blue.

David took two glasses and a bottle of cognac and carried them into the living room.

It was an untidy but homely room. Books and journals were piled on every available surface and jammed into overflowing bookcases. A computer was set up at a desk in one corner of the room. The soft furniture was covered in cream calico and looked comfortable and well used. The lighting was low, with only the side lights switched on. In the mellow glow, the overall impression of the room was cosy and welcoming.

He sat down on the sofa and indicated that she should join him. Pouring them each a generous brandy, he handed one to her.

'Oh, that's good!' Kate felt the burning warmth of the amber liquid trickling down her throat.

David stretched out his long limbs, leaning languorously against the back of the sofa. Reaching for her hand, he entwined his fingers round hers. An unfamiliar heat rose inside her.

'I think I'll take my jacket off,' she said, her face flushed a warm pink. Disengaging his fingers, she stood up and shed her jacket, throwing it over a nearby chair.

As the full sensuality of her black dress, fitting like

a second skin over her slender, rounded figure, was revealed to David for the first time that evening his small inner voice struggled to be heard. Keep away from her, it warned for the hundredth time. Just remember what happened when you got entangled with her family twelve years ago. But the small voice was drowned out by the throbbing, quickening beat of his heart as it responded to the unmistakable feelings of arousal he was now experiencing.

Aware of his eyes on her, Kate ran her hands round the back of her neck and massaged it for a few moments.

'The tension always gets me in the back of the neck. It's probably delayed reaction,' she said. 'It's a pity you're not a physio. I could use a massage right now.'

It was an invitation he could not resist. She had counted on it.

Rising slowing to his feet, he moved behind her and with warm, firm hands gently kneaded and stroked the back of her neck and shoulders till Kate began to feel the tension disappearing. Her whole being was focused on his hands and the exquisite sensation as he worked them expertly over her skin.

Closing her eyes, she let her head roll back against him. Imperceptibly, he unzipped the top few inches of her dress, moving practised hands firmly yet softly along and around her back. His thumbs made circular motions, the tips of his fingers probing and stroking with soporific subtlety on her bare flesh.

His face was in her hair and she could hear his breathing becoming laboured as his comforting touch was now indistinguishable from a caress. What had begun as a medical procedure had turned into something definitely sexual.

Kate felt his hot breath on the back of her neck. With slow fingers he moved her shoulder-length hair to one side.

'You shouldn't be here, you know,' he whispered, his burning lips brushing her skin with tantalising delicacy.

'I'm a grown woman, I know what I'm doing, Dr Firth.' She eased herself against him, luxuriating in his touch.

'Yes, but do *I* know what I'm doing, Dr Marshall?' His hands were sliding down inside her dress, gliding over her silken smooth skin. 'You shouldn't be here,' he repeated. 'Working in this practice, I mean.'

'What are you talking about?' said Kate drowsily, leaning back against his chest.

She was aware that his caresses had ceased, and that his fingers were once again on her zip.

Closing her eyes, she breathed in his arousing masculine scent. However, instead of sliding the fastener down her back, as she'd expected him to, his fingers moved upwards to close the zip.

Still breathing into her hair, he said, 'If I'd known who you were...if I'd been around at the interview...I'd have made sure you didn't get the job.' There was a hard edge to his voice.

Aware that he was no longer jesting, she repeated, 'What are you talking about?'

'You, Dr Marshall, are the last person I would have wanted to join this practice. Even on a temporary basis.'

She was stunned by what she heard. She turned to face him. 'Are you saying I'm no good?'

'Far from it,' he replied, his eyes steely hard in contrast to the softness of his hands, which still stroked her bare neck and shoulders.

'You are an excellent doctor. And why wouldn't you be? You are your father's daughter. But one Dr Marshall trying to ruin my career is enough to last a lifetime.'

He forced himself to stop caressing her silken skin. For God's sake, he told himself once again, keep away! He mustn't allow himself to get any closer. As his eyes flicked over her slender body, her tousled hair, her flushed cheeks, he knew how easy it would be to take her in his arms and— Stop! He mustn't even think about it. He could not, *dared* not, get involved with Kate, however beautiful and desirable she looked at this moment. She was, after all, the daughter of Dr Ewan Marshall, a name that was forever burned on his soul.

He pulled away, releasing her from the warm comfort of his hands. She was shocked to see that his eyes were cool, almost cold.

'Your father tried to destroy me,' he said.

The bitterness in his voice shocked her.

'He forced me to leave medical school. Threatened to have me sent down if I didn't go of my own accord.'

He gave a hollow laugh. 'That man was like a god to me. I admired and respected him, even more than my own father. But your father was a stranger to the truth.' The intensity in his eyes frightened her. 'That man wouldn't know the truth if it jumped up and bit him. He'd much rather take the easy way out, and ruin my career instead.'

Kate was horrified by what he'd said. It was as if she'd been hit by a thunderbolt.

'What on earth are you talking about, David? Are you saying my father tried to ruin your career? *My father?* You must be joking!'

'Do I look as though I'm joking?' He moved away and picked up his brandy with a shaking hand.

Kate was too stunned to speak.

He downed his brandy in one gulp. 'I lost a whole year's medical training because of your father. I suppose it worked out fine in the end because I did become a doctor, in spite of him.'

His voice was calmer now. 'After that I vowed I'd have nothing more to do with your family ever again. And then on Monday you walked in the door.'

Tears stung her eyes.

It was her own father he was saying such terrible things about. It was impossible! She loved her father and knew he could never do anything to hurt another human being. If he had any fault at all, it was a softness where personal relationships were concerned.

That was why he'd married Julia, Kate's stepmother, and had stayed married to her for as long as he had, even though the marriage had obviously been a mistake. In fact, he had only married Julia—a woman who had pursued him mercilessly, Kate realised—in order to give her a mother after her own had died when she was six. Although he'd tried hard to make the marriage work, eventually he'd had to admit failure. Years later, when Kate had been seventeen, he and Julia had gone through a very acrimonious divorce.

Unable to hold back the hot, angry tears that coursed down her cheeks, she brushed them hastily away. She rounded on him accusingly. 'How dare you speak about my father like that? He would never do anything shameful or dishonourable. I think *you* are the one who can't tell the truth!'

Picking up her jacket, she made for the door.

He said nothing, not even looking up as she slammed the door behind her.

CHAPTER FOUR

KATE woke with a frown on her face. She lay in bed without moving, trying to work out the reason for the unease that filled her body. Her alarm clock went off, and at the same moment the previous night's conversation with David came flooding back to her with a sickening rush.

All the implications of his shocking accusations cut through her like a thousand knife wounds. He had said such terrible things about her father, such lies.

Angry with a hard coldness of which she had never thought herself capable, Kate showered and dressed and went downstairs to use the telephone in her surgery.

'You're an early bird,' said her father, delighted to receive a phone call from his daughter, even though it had woken him up. 'Nothing wrong, is there, Kate?'

'No, Dad, nothing at all,' Kate replied quickly, a forced brightness in her voice. 'Dad...I was just wondering... You remember that young student who lived with us about twelve years ago? Was his name David Firth or something like that?' she asked innocently.

'Yes, I believe it was. Why do you ask?' Dr Marshall's voice took on a guarded tone.

'It was just that someone up here reminded me of

him, that's all. I began thinking back to the time when he stayed with us. He left rather suddenly, didn't he? I just can't remember why.' I'd make a very good actress, thought Kate, her calm voice disguising the turmoil inside.

'It was a very unfortunate episode, Kate. Best forgotten.'

'Oh, come on, Dad!' said Kate with artificial jollity. 'You can tell me. I'm a doctor, remember!'

There was an awkward silence at the other end of the phone.

'Dad, for goodness' sake! What's the big secret about David Firth? Now you've whetted my appetite, you've got to tell me!'

'Not over the phone,' said Dr Marshall quietly. 'I'll tell you the whole sorry saga next time we meet.'

Kate could stand the intrigue no longer.

'Actually, I was thinking of coming home at the weekend,' she lied. 'I've a few things I left behind that I need to pick up.'

Dr Marshall was tending his treasured camellias in the front garden of his black-and-white sixteenth-century Cheshire country cottage when Kate arrived from the Lakes.

'Good journey?' he asked, slipping an arm round her shoulders and kissing her fondly on the cheek.

'Door to door in less than ninety minutes,' replied Kate as they strolled in the late spring evening across the lawn towards the house. 'Most of the motorway traffic was going in the opposite direction, thank goodness. Weekend trippers, heading for the mountains.'

Father and daughter chatted amiably as they went inside the house where Dr Marshall now lived on his own. He had never remarried after his divorce from Julia.

Kate was desperate to find out about the mystery surrounding David, but she knew her father well enough to know there would be no rushing him. He would tell her the story in his own time when he felt the moment was right.

Before dinner Dr Marshall had looked tense, his face strained and grey. 'I'll just take a couple of pain-killers before we eat,' he said.

'Still getting those headaches, Dad?' Dr Marshall had suffered from occasional migraines for several years, but he seemed to have been getting them more frequently in recent weeks.

'Nothing to worry about,' he reassured her. 'Probably the excitement of seeing my lovely daughter.'

More likely to be the tension brought on by me mentioning the name of David Firth, thought Kate guiltily.

Dr Marshall broached the subject over coffee.

'That young man was a great disappointment to me,' he began tentatively. 'He was my best student, the one I had most faith in. I trusted him completely. Treated him like a son, even brought him into my own home. And then, after all that, he betrayed me.'

Kate's fingers tightened round the handle of her cup, her knuckles turning white.

'He seemed very nice to me.' That was all she dared venture.

'That's because you were a young girl.' Dr Marshall sounded bitter. 'David Firth was only interested in women, older women. Older women and sex.'

Kate looked at her white-haired father with shocked eyes. Even at sixty, Dr Marshall was a handsome man, but he was a man who could never be described as a womaniser. To hear him talking about women and sex like this made Kate feel decidedly uncomfortable. And Dr Marshall himself looked decidedly uncomfortable, too, as he continued.

'David Firth attempted to seduce your mother.'

Kate's jaw fell open.

'Your stepmother, that is. Julia.' Dr Marshall sipped his coffee, rattling the cup nervously on its saucer. 'That young man took every opportunity to try and get her into bed, and when Julia turned him down he continued to pester her sexually. Julia was too embarrassed to tell me about it at the time because she knew how much I liked David and what a splendid medical student he was.'

'So how did you find out?' Kate was fascinated and horrified at the same time.

'I came home unexpectedly one day—a lecture had been cancelled. I found them together in the bedroom.' Dr Marshall was forcing himself to continue, even though the memory was obviously still very painful for him.

'Julia had no clothes on…on her top half. And they were kissing. Well, David was kissing Julia. Julia was struggling to get away.'

'How dreadful!' Kate was truly shocked at the powerful imagery of David kissing her half-naked stepmother, described in such graphic detail by her father. A tremor ran through her whole body and she had to put down her coffee-cup before she dropped it.

'Julia was distraught,' continued Dr Marshall, his voice now on a more even keel. 'Apparently David had convinced Julia she was a ripe candidate for breast cancer and had insisted on giving her a check-up immediately. Naturally Julia had to strip to the waist in order that he could examine her breasts.

'Once he'd run his disgusting hands all over my wife's breasts, he then pulled her to him and forced his kisses on her. If I hadn't returned home at that precise moment, goodness knows what might have happened. He might very well have raped her.'

Dr Marshall gulped down the last of his coffee. 'It makes me furious to think how the little punk made a fool of a respectable married woman—the wife of his teacher to boot—just to satisfy his lustful instincts.'

'So you made him leave medical school?' Although she knew the answer, Kate still had to hear the full story from her father's lips.

'You bet I did!' retorted Dr Marshall vehemently. 'He was out of the house with his bags packed within the hour.'

'Didn't he deny it?' persisted Kate.

Dr Marshall gave a hollow laugh. 'Of course he did! But, then, he would deny it, wouldn't he? Not only was he a sex maniac, but a liar, too.'

'Do you know what happened to him? Do you know if he became a doctor?' Kate bit her lip nervously.

'No, I don't know what happened to him, Kate, and frankly I don't care.' Dr Marshall put a shaking hand to his head. 'I'm sorry, Kate, but this blasted headache has come back. I'll get an early night and see you in the morning.'

She poured herself another coffee and mulled over the appalling story she had been told that evening. One thing was certain, she knew she could never tell him the terrible truth—that David Firth, sex maniac and liar, was now her medical partner.

As Kate drove back to the Lake District the next evening, the words her father had spoken about David spun round in her head incessantly.

How could she have been so wrong about him, not only when she was a young girl but more recently? And how could someone so intrinsically immoral as David Firth end up as a doctor?

Kate was beginning to lose confidence in her judgement. This was the man who had seemed such an idealist, such a dedicated medical student—and such a dedicated doctor. And all along he'd been a sham, a lustful womaniser prepared to stop at nothing in order to satisfy his uncontrollable sexual urges.

As she left the motorway, the soft contours of the Lake District fells came into view. How very different she felt now from when she had made this same journey just one week ago. Then the magnificent view had lifted her spirits. Now it just filled her heart with apprehension and dismay.

How on earth was she going to get through the next six months? Trying to avoid someone you worked with was difficult enough. How much more difficult it was when you lived with that person in the same house, under the same roof, sharing the same front door.

If Kate was intent on avoiding David, it seemed that he was also intent on avoiding her. She could hear him moving around his flat, and if he did seem to be playing his jazz CDs rather a little too loudly for her comfort she certainly had no intention of telling him to turn them down.

On Monday Kate took over Jenny's patients completely, working on her own now that she'd had a week's gentle introduction to the practice. She was glad to be getting her teeth into the job, and extremely glad not to be shadowing David any more now that she knew the awful truth about him.

Working on her own, throwing herself in at the deep end, was the best possible thing to keep her occupied because when she wasn't completely absorbed in her work she was unable to stop her father's words from returning to haunt her, filling her mind with the dreadful images of David running his hands lustfully over her stepmother's half-naked body.

Kate had a mother-and-baby clinic that morning, something she really enjoyed. It gave Kate a chance to meet some of the local mums as she gave their babies check-ups and inoculations.

'You must have a magic touch,' said one mum, as Kate expertly stabbed the needle into the baby's chubby arm while his attention was distracted by a toy rabbit. 'Damien howled the surgery down last time he had an injection. What's your secret, Dr Marshall?'

'Just a matter of luck, Mrs Thompson,' said Kate

modestly. 'Luck and a fluffy rabbit!' She covered the inoculation site with a small dressing, rubbing it to disperse the serum and to eliminate any needle pain. 'He's a lovely baby,' she said, handing him back to his mother. Baby Damien cooed appreciatively, his tight red curls framing his angelic face so he looked for all the world like a cherub in a pre-Raphaelite painting.

Just before lunch, Gordon chaired the weekly practice meeting in his room. David and Kate greeted each other with polite friendliness, neither of them wishing to alert Gordon to their mutual animosity.

When the general, everyday details of running the practice were out of the way, Gordon mentioned to Kate that he, David and Jenny used this meeting as a forum for airing any diagnostic or clinical problems they had with any of their patients.

'A problem shared, and all that sort of thing,' said Gordon. 'Another opinion can often shine a light where previously there was darkness.' He leaned forward, resting on his hands. 'Actually, I have a particularly puzzling case I'd like to share with you both.'

Gordon went on to describe the symptoms exhibited by one of his patients, a middle-aged, successful businessman who complained of feeling constantly tired and increasingly breathless.

'It's John Marriot. You know him, don't you, David?' continued Gordon. 'He's been a personal friend of mine for many years, as well as being my patient. He's normally as fit as a fiddle, never see him in the surgery from one year to the next. He lives a healthy lifestyle, drinks only in moderation, non-smoker, hillwalker, bit of a fitness freak.

'But for the past year or so he's been a changed man. He's given up hillwalking, can't play squash or tennis, and some days he can hardly drag himself out of bed to go to the office. I've run just about every test I can think of and drawn a blank. And at forty-eight he's not prepared to give up his active life and settle for watching telly all day long. I saw him again this morning. He could hardly drag one foot after the other as he walked into the surgery.'

David and Kate made suggestions, most of which Gordon had already considered and which had proved negative.

'What's his background?' ventured Kate, an idea forming in her mind. 'I mean, has he lived round here all his life or spent some time away?'

'Were you wondering if Marriot has got some mysterious tropical disease?' David said, addressing her directly for the first time during the meeting. 'I don't think he's ever lived abroad, if that's what you had in mind.'

'That wasn't what I had in mind, as a matter of fact,' Kate replied, addressing her next question to Gordon. 'Did Marriot go away to university in his youth, perhaps?'

'Indeed he did,' replied Gordon. 'He's a Cambridge man, as he keeps reminding us whenever they beat Oxford in the boat race.'

'And that would have been in the sixties, wouldn't it?' Kate was doing her mental arithmetic.

'Yes, I suppose it would be around then,' agreed Gordon.

'I really don't see what this has to do with his present condition,' said David, leaning back in his chair.

'It could have a great deal to do with it,' replied Kate. 'I was thinking of hepatitis C.'

'That's an interesting thought,' said Gordon. 'Hepatitis C—a virus that attacks the liver in a much more insidious way than hepatitis A or B.'

'There are several hundred new cases each year, and intravenous drug users are by far the largest group of carriers,' added Kate.

'You're right to consider it, Kate,' said Gordon. 'I just wouldn't have connected hepatitis C with John Marriot—still don't, really. His lifestyle just doesn't point in that direction. He's a top industrialist, a high-flyer—not a drug addict. I'm sure I'd know if he had that kind of problem.' Gordon sounded shaken.

'The symptoms can take years to develop. Twenty or thirty years,' said Kate. 'That's why I asked about his youth and what his lifestyle was then. When I was a junior doctor at the city hospital we saw increasing numbers of cases each week. Many of them were successful professional types who'd had the disease detected when they'd gone for an insurance medical.

'Most of them had no idea how they'd caught it or how long they'd had it. The specialist at the liver unit concluded it must be a legacy from their university days in the ''Swinging Sixties.'' In their youth they might have gone to the occasional wild party and had one or two shots in the arm. It was a long time ago and they've probably forgotten all about it. Now, in their middle age, their past histories are coming back to haunt them.'

'You could just be right,' said David. 'Hepatitis C enters the liver and forces the body's immune system to destroy the infected liver cells. Tiredness and exhaustion will be the first symptoms displayed. In forty or fifty years it can destroy the liver.'

'I'll arrange for Marriot to have a liver biopsy,' said Gordon. 'Good thinking, Kate.' A smile of appreciation, mingled with anxiety for his friend, spread across Gordon's face.

When the meeting broke up Kate left the room first, intending to put as much distance between herself and David as she could. But he crossed the room in half a dozen long strides and they met at the door.

Leaning around her, he reached for the doorhandle. Ever the polite country doctor, mused Kate, desperately trying to fight the sensual feelings that were rising in her, aroused by his closeness.

All through the meeting she had tried to avoid looking at him, aware that her body was reacting in direct opposition to her mind. She felt pulled by two irresistible forces. On the one hand she found him extremely physically attractive; on the other she couldn't bear to let her mind dwell on his past.

As they both stood at the door there was an embarrassing pause. Instead of opening the door, he hesitated for a second, touching her gently on the arm. She could feel his warm breath on her cheek.

'Kate,' he said, 'that was an inspired diagnosis.'

'Thanks.' A pulse beat hard in her throat as she desperately avoided making eye contact with him.

He opened the door and stood back as she walked

ahead of him out of Gordon's room. To her relief he went straight into his own room and shut the door.

Kate didn't see David again until later that evening as he was returning from his house calls. She was opening the front door to her flat when she heard his footsteps on the stairs.

Hurrying to get inside before he could see her, she fumbled with the key, turning it the wrong direction in her anxiety to open the door quickly. 'More haste, less speed,' she muttered to herself crossly. She could hear him coming up the stairs and that made her hand shake even more as she struggled to open the door to her flat.

When he drew level with her he stopped. It was obvious she couldn't avoid talking to him.

'Having trouble?' he asked. 'Here, let me try. Your key is newly cut and sometimes they don't work as well as old ones.'

He seemed to be chattering to cover the discomfort and embarrassment he now appeared to feel being on his own with her. As well he might! thought Kate. I'd feel pretty embarrassed if I'd done what he'd done twelve years ago!

'I saw my father at the weekend,' she blurted out.

She didn't know what had made her say it but once she'd said the words she was glad she'd done so. It had been on her mind constantly and she just had to get it out in the open. She wanted him to know that she *knew*. She knew what kind of person he was.

David appeared not in the least surprised. As the key turned in the door he just remarked, 'I thought you would. What did he say? As if I didn't know.'

Kate pushed past him into the safe haven of her apartment.

'I don't know how you have the bare-faced gall to even talk about it,' she said angrily. 'You behaved like an animal. I'm not surprised my father made you leave medical school. I'd have done the same myself.'

Then she took great satisfaction in slamming the door in his face.

It was in the middle of the night when Kate was woken by the insistent ringing of her mobile phone. Switching on the bedside lamp, she reached out and through bleary eyes managed to pick up the phone and answer the call.

'Dr Marshall speaking.'

'Oh, Doctor, it's Mrs Thompson here. I came to your surgery this morning,' said the anxious voice on the other end of the phone.

'Oh, yes, Mrs Thompson, what can I do for you?' Kate had managed to get her voice and brain quickly into gear. Calls in the middle of the night were something she had become used to from her years on call as a junior hospital doctor. A full night's unbroken sleep was a relatively new luxury in Kate's working life.

'It's Damien, doctor. My baby. You gave him an injection this morning.'

'Yes, I remember. The little boy with the red curls.' Although Kate was fond of children, she didn't get besotted with every baby she saw, but she did admit to finding little Damien particularly attractive. In fact, he was one of the most gorgeous babies she had ever seen, awakening the maternal feelings she tended to push to the back of her mind. Those were a luxury she couldn't afford to indulge in at the moment. One day, maybe, when her career was established. And, of course, when she found the right man to be the father!

'I'm sorry to ring you like this,' Mrs Thompson said apologetically, 'in the middle of the night.' Kate's eyes focused on her bedside clock. It was three o'clock.

'I'm so worried about Damien. He started having terrible attacks of croup earlier this evening. Like really bad whooping cough. He wouldn't eat or drink anything and his temperature is so high. I've put a cold fan in the room, but he's getting no better. My husband's away on business and I'm here on my own. I just don't know what to do, Doctor.'

'Don't worry, Mrs Thompson. Just give me your address and I'll come right away.' Kate wrote down the distraught woman's address. 'Forest Street, number 29. Just keep him cool and I'll be along as soon as I can.'

With years of practice, Kate leapt out of bed and dressed in minutes, pulling sweater and jeans over her short nightdress. It was only as she picked up her doctor's bag and the slip of paper with the address on it that she realised with a sinking feeling she had absolutely no idea where Forest Street was.

There was nothing for it but to ask directions from David no matter how abhorrent she now found it to ask any favours of him. A baby's life could be at risk. She didn't hesitate to do what she had to do.

David answered her urgent knock on his door,

standing barefoot and bare-legged in a navy knee-length bathrobe. His black hair was roughly tousled and dark stubble covered his chin. Kate felt a stab of sexual awareness, realising that even at his most dishevelled David was an extremely attractive man.

Rubbing sleep from his eyes, he was obviously startled to find Kate on his doorstep. Before he could say anything, Kate fired a question at him. 'David, where's Forest Street? I've received an urgent call-out to a 14-month-old baby.'

'Forest Street?' David tried to get his mind into gear. 'Let me think. The best way is to turn left out of our car park, keep going till you reach the T-junction, turn right. Then take the second right…' David paused. He could see the consternation on Kate's face as she tried to fix the directions in her head.

'I'll draw you a map. Come in for minute.' Kate followed him as he went over to his desk and started to draw her a map.

'Right,' he said, handing the sheet of paper to her. 'Hope you can read my writing.' Kate looked with dismay at the indecipherable squiggles.

Seeing the desperation in her eyes, he grabbed the sheet of paper. 'Hang on a minute. I'm coming with you.' David went into his bedroom and dressed speedily, pulling on jeans and sweatshirt in seconds rather than minutes.

'You don't have to, David,' said Kate, with little conviction. 'I'm sure I'll find the house. Eventually.'

David called through the open bedroom door. 'With a baby, time could be of the essence. We must get there quickly. I'd never forgive myself if anything happened just because I went back to bed.'

Kate protested no more. In her heart she felt only relief. Relief that David would be coming along with her. His strong presence was something she desperately needed at that moment. But only on a professional level, she assured herself.

When they arrived at the house, the gratitude on Mrs Thompson's face was touching.

'Thank goodness you came. And not one but two doctors!'

'I'm just the chauffeur this time, Mrs Thompson,' said David. 'Dr Marshall wasn't too sure of the way here.' Kate was glad David had made that point clear to her patient. He could so easily have left the woman with the impression that, as a new young doctor, Kate wasn't to be trusted on her own.

'Is the baby still coughing and wheezing?' asked Kate as they followed Mrs Thompson up the stairs.

'Yes, the croup is still bad. His chest sounds awful. And he has trouble catching his breath sometimes. I moved him into our bedroom so I could keep an eye on him.'

The three adults walked into Mrs Thompson's bedroom. In a drop-sided cot by her bed lay the small, still, almost lifeless figure of Damien, his red curls a damp, tangled mass around his pale face. His eyes were closed, the eyelids blue, his breathing shallow and irregular.

As Kate leaned over the little body the baby began to cough, drawing in breaths which rattled and grated with a heart-stopping sound, racking his small chest.

She examined him with her stethoscope and took

his temperature, then looked at David with concern. 'I think we'd better get Damien straight to hospital. It's most likely a bad reaction to the inoculation I gave him earlier today. I don't think we can take any chances. And I don't think we've any time to lose.'

David nodded, agreeing with her diagnosis. Instantly he was on his mobile phone, calling the hospital for an emergency ambulance and then speaking to the paediatrician.

'We're sending along an emergency, 14-month-old baby boy, Damien Thompson. Possible post-inoculation reaction.'

Turning to the anxious mother, he said, 'And don't worry, Mrs Thompson. If the ambulance isn't here in five minutes, Dr Marshall and I will drive you to the hospital ourselves.'

Less than twenty minutes later, Kate and David were back home, walking from the car to the practice in the eerie stillness of early morning.

The ambulance had arrived speedily at the Thompsons' house and the paramedics had taken mother and sick baby to hospital.

Kate shivered involuntarily in the cool, crisp air.

'I'm sure the baby will be all right,' David said confidently. 'You got there in time and made the right decision to hospitalise him straight away.'

'I hope so,' said Kate, as they let themselves into the house. 'He was such a bonny baby this morning before I gave him the inoculation. He hardly looked like the same child just now, so ill and dehydrated.'

'He's in the best hands.'

'I know...but...' Kate suddenly felt very emotional. 'But he's not out of the woods yet. He's still in a life-threatening situation, and...' Kate felt tears sting her eyes and hastily brushed them away. 'I expect you think me soppy and sentimental to get upset about a baby like this.'

'Not at all,' said David gravely. 'I've been known to shed tears myself where my small patients are involved. We can't always act the cool, uninvolved professional. Sick children have an uncanny way of insinuating themselves into your thoughts and breaking through the barriers we medics erect around ourselves.'

They were now outside Kate's flat. Kate was completely drained, emotionally and physically. As if in a trance she searched around for the keys which she located in her jeans pocket. David took them.

'Here, let me,' he said firmly. 'You seem to have trouble opening this door.'

The door swung open under his deft touch. Kate pushed past him, wishing to be out of his disturbing presence as quickly as possible for, although she felt revolted by his past behaviour, whenever she was physically close to him she also felt something else—an animal magnetism that radiated from him. And the closer she was to him, the stronger she felt it. Sometimes the very closeness of him made her feel dizzy, her emotions swinging pendulum-like between extremes of loathing and desire.

She went inside, quickly closing the door behind her. Leaning against the back of the door, she found she was trembling. Why did she want him so much? A man like that! A man who had nearly raped her stepmother.

Pulling off her jeans and sweater, she crawled back into the crumpled bed, and even though she was longing for sleep she dreaded it, knowing for certain she would dream of David, as she had dreamed of him every night since he had stroked and caressed the back of her neck with such tenderness...the night she had imagined he would take her in his arms and kiss her.

Her dreams were so vivid she woke up damp with perspiration, able to recall every lurid detail. Although during the daytime hours she could follow the dictates of her head, when she was asleep she became a helpless bystander as her body betrayed her, finding sensual relief in dreams of passionate fantasy.

CHAPTER FIVE

NEXT morning, fresh from the shower, Kate breakfasted at the small table in her kitchen on black coffee and rolls heated up in the oven.

She'd managed to grab two or three hours' sleep before her alarm went off. Considering her broken night, she felt surprisingly fresh and alert. Mindless music was coming out of the portable radio, the station deliberately chosen to banish all waking thoughts of David. But, try as she might, she couldn't get him out of her mind.

She was becoming worryingly obsessed with the man. He exuded sexual attraction—there was no other explanation for her fixation. Is that how he gets his way with women? Is that how he seduced Julia?

Last night her emotional feelings about baby Damien had made her drop her guard against David. His concern for the baby, showing her the softer side of his nature, had all been an act put on for her benefit. It had had the desired effect, making her think of him as a normal, attractive man. But that was just what he wasn't. She must be on her guard constantly for the next six months, otherwise she would find herself drawn into his web. To be taken in by this most unprincipled man would be the height of irresponsibility on her part.

Any sexual longings she had for David Firth must be kept securely buried in her heart.

* * *

A week passed. And then another. The good days outnumbered the bad. There was good news about Damien, now back home and thriving as if his brush with death had never happened.

Kate threw herself into her work, determined to be the best GP the Lake District had ever known. All three doctors worked in harmony, pooling ideas and discussing particularly interesting patients and cases. Kate was extremely gratified one day when Gordon told her that, following a liver biopsy, her suggested diagnosis of hepatitis C for John Marriot had been proved correct.

To her relief, in office hours at least, David acted with clinical detachment towards her. This was mainly due, Kate surmised, because she had made sure that she was never alone with him. Every spare moment when she wasn't working was filled with activity. She joined a local hillwalking group and took up Jean's open invitation to 'pop in any time'. Gordon's wife, although several years older than Kate, had a similar sense of humour and she and Kate spent many a happy hour together.

After Kate had been in the Lakes a month she had planned to spend the next weekend at home with her father, but at the last minute she had to cancel as she was on call on the Saturday. She rang her father to apologise for changing the arrangements.

'Don't worry,' he said. 'I'd also forgotten that I'd made an appointment with the optician, and it saves me changing the day if you're not coming up.'

'Is it time for a new eye test already, Dad?' asked Kate. 'I thought you got new bifocals only six months ago.'

'I did,' confirmed Dr Marshall. 'I just don't think they're any good, that's all. They give me double vision.'

'Double vision?' Kate clutched the phone a little tighter than usual. 'You never told me about that.'

'Nothing to worry about. New bifocals will sort it out.'

'And how are the headaches?' she asked.

'About the same. I think I need some stronger painkillers.' His voice gave nothing away.

'If the headaches are about the same,' persisted Kate, 'why do you need stronger painkillers?' A tiny prickle of concern was forming in her mind.

'Do stop fussing, girl,' said Dr Marshall with uncharacteristic sharpness.

'I've got a funny call on one of the lines,' said Tracy, cupping her hand over the phone. Kate was walking past at the time, on her way out to lunch. She had her mind set on an ice-cool lemonade, a fresh salmon sandwich and a chat with Pat, the landlady of the Hare and Hounds and a fellow member of Kate's hillwalking group.

Tracy beckoned her over.

'Is it a heavy breather?' ventured Kate.

'I'm not sure. It's a sort of cross between a heavy breather and a midget.' Tracy giggled and handed the phone to Kate. Intrigued, Kate listened.

A small quavery voice said, 'She won't wake up'. Then there came the sound of someone breathing very close to the phone.

'Who's speaking?' asked Kate authoritatively. She

heard a sharp intake of breath at the other end of the line.

'It's Wob,' said the squeaky, midget-sized voice.

'Wob?' repeated Kate.

'Wob. Wobert.'

'Oh, Robert! And how old are you, Robert?' asked Kate gently.

'Free.'

'Three?'

'Yes.'

Kate turned to Tracy. 'It's not an obscene call. It's a little boy called Robert, who's three. I'll find out what he wants.'

Speaking into the phone again. 'What do you want, Robert?'

'Mummy. Mummy won't wake up.' The little voice sounded frightened.

Kate said urgently in an aside to Tracy, 'Get one of the other doctors to come here straight away. It could be a medical emergency.'

'David's still in,' said Tracy, leaping into action. 'He's not out on his rounds yet.'

Kate spoke slowly into the phone. 'Right, Robert. Just tell me what has happened. Where's Mummy now?'

'She's...she's sleeping on the floor. She won't wake up... She told me to press this button on the phone and then she fell down on the floor and went to sleep.'

David had responded to Tracy's call for help and was standing at Kate's elbow. 'What is it?' he asked calmly.

Kate covered the phone. 'It's a little boy called

Robert. He's three and his mother is lying unconscious on the floor. He seems to have pressed a pre-programmed telephone button which connected him to the surgery.'

'Ask him his surname and where he lives,' asked David. 'We can send someone round.'

'Robert,' said Kate gently, 'What is your surname?'

The voice at the other end started to quaver again, and Kate realised he was about to start crying. 'What's your second name, Robert?' she said, hoping to simplify the request.

'Wobert. My name's Wobert,' he squeaked.

'Yes, but what's your other name, Robert?'

'Wobert, just Wobert.' He sniffed.

'You must have another name,' persisted Kate.

'I haven't, I haven't!' he wailed, blubbing into the phone. Oh, God, thought Kate, he's only three and he has no idea what his surname is.

'Don't cry, Robert, be a brave boy.' Kate tried again. 'Where do you live, Robert?'

'In the Lake Distwick,' he replied with childlike simplicity.

'But where?'

'It's the house with the black fluffy cat next door. Do you know it?'

'It's a house with a black fluffy cat next door,' said Kate to the others, raising her eyes in silent exasperation. Tracy giggled.

In desperation Kate tried another line of questioning. 'What's the name of the road where the cat is?'

'I don't know.' He sounded so miserable and dejected. It was as if he knew, even at three, that it was terribly important that he should know the name of his road, but as nobody had ever told him what it was they might as well be asking him about the theory of relativity.

'We're getting nowhere here,' said Kate desperately to David. 'Assuming the family are patients of ours, do you know any family with a little boy called Robert?'

'With a practice the size of ours, there could be quite a lot.' David thought for a moment. 'We've just started putting all the patients' medical files on our new computer. Keep the kid on the phone while I search through the files. This is one occasion when a computer programme should be superior to a real doctor going through the medical records by hand.'

Kate managed to calm the little boy and stop him from putting the phone down. She established that his mother wasn't bleeding.

'Sounds as though she's in some sort of coma,' Kate called through to where David was working on the computer. 'Check all the patients with epilepsy, diabetes, hypertension and…' Good grief, thought Kate, a coma could be caused by any number of conditions or illnesses.

After what seemed an eternity but was, in fact, only minutes, David called through to Kate, 'I've got something here. A new family, just moved into the area and the wife is a diabetic. There are three children, aged eight, six and three—called Jason, Liza and Robert.'

Grasping at the straw, Kate said to Robert, 'Do you have a big brother called Jason? And a sister called Liza?'

'Yes!' he said, shrieking with delight. 'Jason and Liza are at big school. I'm going to big school next year!'

'I think we've cracked it,' called Kate with relief to David. 'We'll be round at your house in a few minutes, Robert. You just keep talking on the phone to Tracy, the nice lady who is standing next to me, and I'll be at your house to look after Mummy as quickly as I can.'

She handed the phone to Tracy. 'Keep him talking till we arrive, and then tell him to let us in.'

Only pausing to pick up their bags and to phone for an ambulance, Kate and David ran towards the car park. 'I just had a thought,' said Kate. 'I hope he's tall enough to reach the front doorknob!'

'That won't stop me getting in,' said David, sliding into his car seat next to Kate and starting the engine. 'I've broken down doors before now to get where I want to be.'

'Yes,' said Kate with ill-disguised sarcasm, 'I'm sure you have.'

'You must be the cleverest, bravest little boy in the whole Lake District,' said Kate with genuine admiration, hugging the three-year-old to her. 'I wouldn't be surprised if your picture is in the paper next week, saying ROBERT JOHNSON SAVES HIS MUMMY'S LIFE!'

The flaxen-haired child giggled uncontrollably at the thought. 'Wait till I tell Daddy!' He laughed happily, climbing onto Kate's knee and flinging his little arms round her neck.

Who would have thought this was the same child

who'd reached up on tiptoe to open the front door to them less than twenty minutes ago? Then, his stricken, anxious face had had fear written all over it as he'd led the two doctors into the sitting room where his mother had lain unconscious on the floor.

'Make Mummy wake up,' he'd kept repeating in a small, frightened voice.

David and Kate had knelt down by the woman whose breathing had been deep and laboured, a faint smell of acetone lingering on her breath. 'Hypoglycaemia,' they'd said at the same moment, instantly recognising the very distinctive signs of diabetic attack. David had checked her pulse, 'It's racing,' he'd said. 'We'd better check her BM then we'll know how much glucose to give intravenously.'

Kate pricked Mrs Johnson's finger, smearing the spot of blood onto a special strip of paper which she placed on the portable machine that would give an instant readout of her blood sugar level.

'Her glucose level is one,' said Kate.

'No wonder she's in a hypo coma,' said David, preparing the glucose syringe with speed and dexterity. David then gave Mrs Johnson the injection.

Kate, meanwhile, was comforting Robert, holding the little boy in a gentle, rocking embrace, reassuring him about his mother. 'She'll be fine, Robert. Dr Firth will make her better.'

David gave Kate a sideways glance. 'Thank you for that vote of confidence, Dr Marshall,' he said sarcastically, a cynical smile twisting his lips.

Damn the man, reacted Kate. Even at a time like this, in the middle of a medical emergency, he can penetrate my inner being and disturb me like no other man ever could.

Kate dropped her eyes and hugged Robert to her fiercely. 'Mummy will be better soon,' she promised.

The glucose worked with magical speed and within seconds the woman on the floor began to stir.

'Mrs Johnson,' said David. 'Wake up, Mrs Johnson, open your eyes.' He kept speaking to her, coaxing her back to consciousness. 'Can you hear me, Mrs Johnson? Open your eyes. Open them now.'

Mrs Johnson opened her eyes and instantly tried to sit up. David helped her as she slowly came round and took in the situation.

'I'd just like to test your glucose level again, Mrs Johnson.' He squeezed another spot of blood from her finger and repeated the finger-prick test. The machine now registered a reading of seven. David and Kate seemed satisfied with this result.

Robert ran to his mother with a delighted whoop. 'Mummy! Mummy! Are you better now? It was just like Sleeping Beauty. I thought you would sleep for a hundred years!'

Kate, David and Mrs Johnson laughed spontaneously at Robert's interpretation of his mother's diabetic coma.

'Sleeping Beauty wakes up when a handsome prince kisses her,' the little boy babbled on. He was now so excited and relieved there was no stopping him.

Mrs Johnson smiled at Dr Firth. 'Well, this handsome prince just gave me an injection,' she said with a laugh. 'I don't think Daddy would be too pleased if he'd tried to revive me with a kiss!'

David joined in the light-hearted banter. 'No, in your Mummy's case a glucose injection was the first thing to try. The kiss of life would have been my second option!' The sound of a siren interrupted them.

'That'll be the ambulance we phoned for from the surgery,' said Kate. 'I'll let them in.' She went out of the house into the front garden and waved at the ambulance, which was just turning the corner into the Johnson's road.

The paramedics came into the house and had a short discussion with the two doctors and Mrs Johnson.

'I know the medical emergency is over, Mrs Johnson,' said David, 'but I really think you should let these gentlemen take you to hospital for a thorough check-up.'

'I don't need to go to hospital.' Mrs Johnson was adamant. 'I can't leave Robert, and my two other children will be home from school in an hour or two. It just isn't practical. Anyway,' she persisted, 'there's nothing wrong with me now, apart from the diabetes.'

David and Kate could see the woman was determined to stay at home.

'Can't you ask a neighbour to look after your children?' David asked.

'We're new around here,' she replied. 'I don't really know anyone that I'd feel happy leaving the children with. And I know once they get me into hospital it could be days before I get home—all those tests they'll keep wanting to do. Besides, there's really nothing wrong with me. Well, there wasn't until they changed my insulin prescription. I've had diabetes since I was a teenager and always managed perfectly well with the insulin I injected. I never once went into a coma and I had adequate warning signs if my blood sugar level was dropping.'

David raised his eyebrows in interest. 'I see from your records you used to be on the old-style insulin,' he said, looking at Mrs Johnson's file. 'The sort extracted from the pancreas of a pig. More recently, your last GP prescribed the newer product, derived from human insulin. Are you saying the change hasn't suited you?'

With David's help Mrs Johnson stood up and moved over to a chair. 'It most certainly does not suit me,' she said emphatically, 'but my previous doctor told me to give it a further trial.'

'So today isn't the first time you've had problems with lapsing into a coma?' enquired David.

'I've had a hypo attack twice before,' answered Mrs Johnson. 'Fortunately each time previously it was in the evening when my husband was at home. He injected me straight away and I soon came round. But it gave me a fright and since then I've been worried sick it will happen again, like it did just now. Thank goodness Robert had the presence of mind to press the short-dial button. I only programmed the surgery number in a few days ago. I mean, imagine if I'd been driving at the time? Taking the children to school?' She shuddered. 'It just doesn't bear thinking about.'

David turned to the paramedics. 'Thanks for coming but I think we can dispense with your services this time. I'll take responsibility for my patient. I'm sure she's right when she says it's just a matter of adjusting her insulin programme and I can sort that out with her now.'

When the ambulance had driven away, David returned to the subject of Mrs Johnson's insulin.

'I'm very sorry that the human insulin doesn't seem to suit you, Mrs Johnson. There have been a few reports of similar problems, both here and in America. The laboratory-produced human insulin is supposedly a much better product, but in a few isolated cases there have been side-effects—headaches, feeling unwell and, more worrying, no warning of a sudden drop in blood sugar levels, resulting in coma.

'What I'd like to do is to make you an appointment with a specialist, an endocrinologist, who can update and revise your insulin programme. You really shouldn't be having problems like this. Treating diabetes is one of medicine's success stories.' David pulled out a prescription pad. 'In the meantime, I'll write you a prescription for the old type of insulin, the one you had no problems with.' Tearing it off, he handed her the note.

'Thank you, Doctor.' She turned to Kate, who seemed to have made a friend for life in Robert, his little arms clutching her neck so tightly she thought she'd choke. 'And thank you, Doctor. Come on, Robert, let the doctors go now and look after other sick people. Really sick people, not just someone like me. I feel a bit of a fraud, causing so much fuss over such a simple thing.'

'It's not simple at all, Mrs Johnson,' rejoined Kate. 'It could have been very serious if you hadn't had such a clever little boy to come to your aid. You can be very proud of Robert. He didn't panic for a moment, just spoke calmly to us and told us what was going on.'

Mrs Johnson held her arms open for Robert, who ran to her. 'Thank you, darling. You saved Mummy's life,' she said, tears brimming in her eyes.

'Mummy,' he said, snuggling up to her, 'what's my other name?'

Mrs Johnson looked puzzled. 'It's Johnson, Robert Johnson. Didn't you know that?'

'No,' he said crossly. 'They kept asking me and I didn't know. You never told me. So I couldn't tell them. But I told them about the fluffy black cat,' he added proudly. 'That's probably how they found us.'

'You can drop me here,' said Kate breezily as they approached the Hare and Hounds. 'I'm just popping in for a bite of lunch. No doubt you're off on your rounds. Mustn't keep the patients waiting.'

David stopped the car outside the pub and switched off the engine. 'You seem in an awful hurry to get away from me. I know you've been avoiding me. Don't think I haven't noticed.'

'I don't know what you're talking about,' said Kate with false confidence. 'I thought we had a very good professional relationship.'

'That's not what I'm talking about, as you well know. You've been like this ever since you had that little heart-to-heart with your father. I might have known he'd tell you a pack of lies—or at least his own very slanted version of the story.'

Kate bristled. 'He told me *everything,*' she snapped. 'I know everything about you and your morals and, all things considered, I think I'm putting up a pretty good attempt at working with you, knowing what I know.'

'Then I can only assume you know nothing, otherwise you'd have realised it was all a terrible misunderstanding,' he snapped back. 'You're more like your father than I feared.'

'What's that supposed to mean?' Kate was stiff with fury.

'I had hoped you'd approach the issue with an open mind,' he replied calmly.

'My father told me what happened. It's as simple as that. And I believed him.'

'Then that makes two of you with closed minds.'

'I don't have to sit here and let you accuse me of having a closed mind.' Kate turned to open the car door but David was too quick for her. In a split second he had pressed the central-locking device. The passenger door remained firmly shut.

'Not only do you have a closed mind, you're also afraid of me, aren't you?' His eyes burned into her accusingly.

'What rubbish!' she said, tilting her chin defiantly.

'You're afraid to be alone with me.' His voice was very calm and level.

'I am not.'

'Then prove it,' he challenged. 'Come out with me tonight. To dinner.'

'All right,' she said, tossing her head in the air. 'Just to prove I've an open mind.'

He released the door lock and put his hand back on the steering-wheel, sensing victory. 'I'll pick you up at eight,' he said dispassionately.

As he drove away Kate sighed resignedly. Oh, God, she thought with a wince, what have I let myself in for? What am I doing, getting involved with this man?

She walked into the pub, already knowing the answers to her own questions. She was getting involved with David Firth because she couldn't help herself. She couldn't help herself any more than a drowning sailor caught up in a whirlpool could help himself. Slowly and surely she was being sucked down into the vortex. Down and down and into his arms, and probably into his bed.

A tremor ran through her as she visualised David's naked body next to hers, his mouth on her skin, his strong hands touching her, pleasuring her…

'Lime and lemonade, please, Linda,' she said when she got to the bar, 'with lots and lots of ice.'

Got to have something to cool me down, thought Kate desperately. Something to take my mind off the unthinkable. Unthinkable maybe, but undeniably what her treacherous body craved.

At five minutes to eight, Kate was standing at one of the tall windows, looking out as the sun slipped behind the mountains, bathing them in the golden light of a perfect summer's evening.

No other place in England could have such incredible beauty as here in the Lakes, thought Kate, such perfection of form and colour, with the mountains, water and trees blending together in such supreme harmony.

After her surgery and house calls, Kate had had a long soak in the bath to relax and unwind, determined to get herself into the right frame of mind for the evening ahead.

What should she wear? she'd mused, relaxing in the scented foam. David hadn't specified what kind of restaurant he would be taking her to. It could be anything from a cheap-and-cheerful pizzeria to a full-blown, expensive fancy restaurant. Better not to wear jeans. A dress? she'd pondered as she'd lifted the plug with her toe, allowing the water to escape the bath. Yes, she'd wear a dress. Well, that had made the choice simple enough. She only had two.

Having had little enough time during her training years for a decent social life, Kate hadn't wasted her money on evening clothes. She did have a couple of smart suits, hastily bought before taking up this locum job. They were clothes she'd hoped would make her look older and be more in keeping with the patients' image of a doctor.

Otherwise her wardrobe consisted mainly of comfortable short skirts and jeans which had the effect of making Kate, with her slim figure and fresh complexion, look about sixteen years old. Hardly the vision to inspire patients with confidence in her medical skills.

She had the sleeveless, figure-hugging little black number she'd worn to supper at Gordon's and Jean's in her first week. And she had one other dress, a filmy, midnight blue chiffony affair with a scoop neck and a skirt that reached to her knees, floating sexily round her legs as she walked.

Pulling it out of the wardrobe, she'd held it against her. It had long, see-through sleeves and wasn't quite as revealing as the black.

Slipping it on over her lace bra and pants, she'd watched with satisfaction as the gossamer silky chiffon had fallen in soft folds over her shapely breasts and rounded hips. She'd stood back and had taken a critical look at herself in the mirror. Everything had come together well—the striking deep blue dress, her golden hair, her long legs in delicate, French navy high-heeled shoes.

The midnight blue of the dress perfectly matched her eyes and seemed to make her hair shine even brighter than usual. She'd clasped a thick, solid gold rope necklace round her throat, touching it appreciatively as she did every time she wore it. It was the only piece of jewellery she owned or wanted, and it was very special to her.

It had belonged to her mother, her real mother, who had died when Kate was six. Kate had a vague memory of seeing her wearing it, at least she thought she did. It might have been all in her mind, wanting so much to remember her real mother and not wanting to forget, even though there had been another woman who had tried to take her mother's place less than a year later. Julia. Julia, whom Dr Marshall had hoped would be a good wife and mother. It had been this desperate hope which had led him to make such a dreadful mistake in ever marrying her in the first place.

Reflecting on her childhood, Kate recalled that the relationship between her and Julia had been more like that of sisters rather than mother and child. Kate's stepmother, several years younger than her husband, had wanted Kate to call her Julia, not Mummy. It had actually been very confusing for the young Kate because her father, longing to recreate the close family unit, had insisted on referring to Julia as 'your mother'.

Her father had kept many aspects of his remarriage from Kate, seeking solace in his teaching. It had only been around the time of the divorce that Kate had caught a brief insight into their true relationship, having overheard a heated conversation between them.

'You never really loved me, Julia. I was just a trophy for your collection,' she heard her father saying bitterly. 'That's not true,' protested her glamorous stepmother. 'I certainly fancied you. I fancied you a lot.'

'What you fancied, Julia, was being the wife of a professor. Status, that's what you married me for. In that case,' snapped Julia, 'we *each* got what we wanted out of the marriage. Face it, Ewan, all you wanted was a mother for Kate and I've fulfilled that part of the bargain.'

Bringing her thoughts back to the present, Kate was glad she had allowed herself plenty of time to get ready for this date with David. She hadn't relished the thought of him arriving early and sending her into a panic just when she'd managed to calm herself down with a soothing bath.

She was still gazing out of the window, watching the play of the dying sunlight on the mountain ridges, when, dead on eight, she heard his firm rap on the door.

She opened it. He said nothing, his grey eyes glancing over her, taking in every detail of her dress.

He practically undresses you with his eyes, thought Kate, reacting to his scrutiny.

'Will I need a jacket, do you think?' asked Kate briskly, before shutting her door.

'No,' he replied, leading the way down the stairs. 'We're going straight to the restaurant and there's parking right outside.'

They drove out of the village, skirting a lakeside forest and, with their backs to the setting sun, sped cross country past farm buildings and fields bounded by dry-stone walls. After about five miles they came to a large country house set back from the road. David turned his Range Rover into the drive, the wheels crunching on the grey stone gravel.

'We're not the first here,' said Kate as they parked alongside six other cars.

'Danilo's is a popular place,' said David. 'We were lucky to get a table at such short notice. But Danny, the proprietor, is a good friend of mine.'

He would be, thought Kate. I bet you use your charm to get your way with everybody.

He jumped out and opened her door, his hand under her elbow, helping her out. He was standing very close to the car, leaving her little room to step onto the gravel without pressing up close against him, which was obviously his intention.

His grip tightened on her waist, the warmth of his hand searing through the thin chiffon of her dress. 'You're looking lovely tonight, Kate.'

Before she could react he'd stepped back from her, shutting and locking the car door in one smooth movement.

As they walked into the restaurant Kate, for the first time that evening, studied him carefully. The lean, hip-hugging, well-cut trousers. The beautifully tailored light grey jacket. The black hair brushed sleekly back. Whether in his role as country doctor, mountain rescuer or, as tonight, dressed to kill, David managed to look exactly the part.

What a smooth operator. The voice in her head told her to beware, but the beating of her heart drowned out the voice of reason.

Over the candlelit dinner, Kate let herself be drawn even closer into his web, as she'd known she would be. Not that he touched her or talked in a particularly intimate way. It was as though he was biding his time, toying with her, playing with her.

He ordered the meal and wine with the ease and confidence of a man well used to that kind of lifestyle. No doubt he takes many women out to dinner, surmised Kate, all part of his softening-up process.

She took another sip of the Chianti Classico.

A chilling thrill ran through her. In that same instant she realised that she wanted him as much as he, quite obviously, wanted her.

Kate had long been aware there was a deeply sensual streak in her. It was just unfortunate that it was now, and with this most unsuitable man, that the erotic side of her nature should have been awakened so violently and with such intensity. It was all so…inconvenient.

She studied him across the guttering candles. The line of his jaw was strong and firm, his mouth generous, the roughened lips surprisingly sensual for such a masculine face.

His voice, huskily low, seemed to be caressing her and stroking her, stoking the fires of her libido, without him even having to lay a finger on her.

What would her father think if he could see her now? How disgusted he would be, how shocked and disappointed in her. It was as if freezing water had been thrown over her, causing her to shudder.

'Not cold, are you?' he asked, breaking off what he was saying.

She shook her head. 'Please, go on. I'm very interested in hearing about your family. You seem to know so much about mine—even though we disagree about the interpretation.' She smiled a calculating smile. Two could play at his game of cat and mouse.

He topped up her glass with the last of the Chianti.

He smiled at her. He'd been smiling at her a lot this evening. No doubt he believed he'd got a lot to smile about, anticipating the night ahead.

'So, that's just about it, as far as my life story goes. Father a doctor in the army, with constant postings abroad, resulting in boarding school for his two sons. We had terrific school holidays in exotic places, but never really felt we belonged anywhere. Living in the Lake District for these past three years has been the closest I've come to having a home base. It also connects quite nicely with my roots, if I have any, because this is where I was conceived.'

Kate laughed. 'Really?'

'On one of my father's home leaves my parents spent a holiday in the Lakes. My older brother was staying with our grandparents, and so it was like a second honeymoon for them. I was born nine months later.'

'How romantic!' she said delightedly.

'It certainly was. I began life, in the biological sense of the word, in a very romantic little place, overlooking Lakeland's deepest lake, Wast Water, in the shadow of the country's tallest mountain, Scafell Pike.'

He reached across the table. For the first time, since coming into the restaurant, he touched her hand, moving his long fingers lightly over hers with gentle, caressing strokes. Even that slight touch sent shivers down her spine.

'I'll take you there one day,' he said, his voice deep and husky. 'That is, if you like strenuous hill-walking. Scafell is not for the faint-hearted.'

When they left the restaurant a short time later they were greeted by a wall of mist that swirled around in the light escaping from the restaurant. Kate shuddered with the sudden drop in temperature, hugging her arms to keep warm.

'Wish I'd brought my jacket now.' Her teeth were chattering.

David took off his jacket and slipped it round her shoulders, putting an arm round her as they quickened their pace to the car.

'This is so typical of Lake District weather,' said David resignedly. 'One minute it's a beautiful sunny day, the next it's damp and cold and misty. It's so unpredictable. As many a hillwalker discovers to his cost.'

Even inside the car Kate was still cold. 'I just can't believe the change in such a short time. It's as cold as winter now.'

He put the key in the ignition but didn't start the engine straight away. Instead, he slid his arm round the back of her seat and pulled her to him. 'I'll warm you up.'

In the dark, intimate atmosphere of the car, with the mist swirling round outside, Kate felt safe and secure in his arms. How good it felt, the heat from his body permeating through to hers. And deep inside a relaxed drowsiness began to take hold. The food and the wine, particularly the wine, was beginning to take effect.

With a contented sigh she pressed closer to him, languorously leaning her head on his shoulder. She could feel his body, muscular and hard. He stroked her hair, moving with gentle fingers the strands that had fallen over her eyes. Running his hand under her chin, he lifted her face to his.

'What is it about you that enslaves me?' he said hoarsely. 'Sitting across the table from you this evening, it was torture. You looked so beautiful, so desirable. I wanted so much to touch you and kiss you. Like this.'

His hands clasped her face, holding her head captive. She could see his face dimly in the shadows, his dark eyes glittering in the light from the restaurant as his mouth came down on hers, fiercely, hungrily. Ruthlessly he forced her lips apart, invading her mouth with a rough urgency. The intensity of his passion took her unawares and she gasped for air, feeling she would be suffocated, so helpless was she in his grip.

She closed her eyes and kissed him back, trembling violently as his hand moved down from her face, down her throat and over her breast. She gasped again, this time not for air but out of pleasure, drawing in her breath sharply as she felt her nipples harden under his touch.

His mouth slid hotly down her neck, making her shudder with excitement. She moaned, twisting her body closer to his. 'Oh, David.' It was all she could say, breathless with desire.

'I want you, Kate,' he whispered thickly. 'I wanted you the first moment I set eyes on you in the surgery waiting room, and I thought to myself, Oh, hell, she's a patient so that's the end of that. Unless, of course, I wanted to end up in front of the general medical council.'

He moved his hand away from her breast. 'Let's get home. If we stay here much longer we'll get arrested for indecency. Anyway, it's more comfortable at home.' He didn't add 'in bed'. He didn't have to. His meaning was perfectly clear. Kissing her lightly on the forehead, he started the engine.

Kate was now wide wake, fully aroused and alert, having been shaken out of her comfortable lethargy. She buckled her seat belt and tried to think straight.

I've fallen into his trap. I'm like a ripe peach, just waiting to be eaten. A ripe peach he thinks he can pick up any time he chooses. And, of course, he's right. Kate had to admit the truth, hating herself for it. This man is like a drug. A drug that gives so much pleasure you want more, and more. Even though you know it will harm you in the end. He's taken me to the brink and pulled back, knowing I'm primed for the next time.

The journey home took much longer than the outward journey earlier that evening now that the mountain mist had blanketed the countryside like a white-out. It was almost impenetrable with visibility virtually down to nil, forcing David to drive extremely slowly, with the fog lamps on.

One good thing about the long journey, as far as Kate was concerned, was the fact that it forced her to confront the developing relationship between herself and David. It was all very well lusting after this man, but what about the future? How on earth could she explain to her father if he ever found out? Especially now he had told her the awful truth about his former medical student.

By the time they reached the tall stone house, Kate had pulled herself together and had decided not to give in to her baser instincts. She wouldn't go to bed with him, she told herself soberly. Just think about him and Julia. Just think of him kissing her, touching her, fondling her breasts. Surely, thought Kate firmly, that's enough to make any decent person feel sick. Stiffening her resolve, she took a deep breath. Now she felt composed enough to cope with the situation.

Having parked the car, David switched off the engine and was about to turn to her when his mobile phone rang. It made Kate jump—the phone was in the inside pocket of David's jacket which was still round her shoulders. She handed it to him. 'Didn't know you were on call tonight.'

'I'm not. Probably a wrong number.'

It was so still and quiet in the car that Kate could hear both sides of the telephone conversation. The call was from someone called Gareth and it was about a mountain rescue.

An inexperienced walker was stuck on the hills with what sounded like a broken ankle. His companion had struggled down through the mist and raised the alarm.

'We're setting out at first light to try and find him,' said Gareth. 'Are you able to come with us, David?'

'Count me in,' said David briskly. 'Usual meeting place?'

'Yes,' answered Gareth, 'the youth hostel car park. At 5 a.m.'

David turned off the mobile. 'Looks like our romantic evening has come to an abrupt halt.'

Kate smiled to herself. You may not realise it, but your romantic evening came to an abrupt halt some time ago, Dr Firth.

'I'd better try and get a few hours' kip before the rescue,' he said.

Kate unbuckled her seat belt and sat up, thinking hard for a moment. 'Let me come with you,' she ventured. 'I've done quite a bit of hillwalking, got all the gear, and they may be glad of another medic.'

'Are you sure?' He was taken aback by her offer, but nevertheless gratified. 'The more volunteers, the better—especially on a case like this when there's an inexperienced walker who has no idea where he is. His companion was very vague as to where he had left him, so we could need two or three teams of searchers, covering a wide area. Can you be ready at 4:45 a.m.?'

'Of course,' confirmed Kate, jumping out of the car with enthusiasm.

They walked towards the house together. He smiled at her companionably. 'Doesn't look as though we'll be getting much sleep tonight with such an early start.' He paused, taking out his front door key.

'Pity about the mountain rescue,' he said regretfully. 'I can think of much nicer ways of not getting much sleep. Another night maybe.'

She turned to go to her own flat. 'Maybe,' she replied casually.

Just don't count your chickens, David Firth, that's all.

CHAPTER SIX

IT WAS hardly daylight when they drove into the youth hostel car park. The temperature had fallen further during the night, the mist still hung around patchily and there were signs of a ground frost.

Both David and Kate were well clothed against the cold weather in warm waterproof trousers, sweaters, thermal fleece tops and waterproof jackets. Kate's leather walking boots weren't as well worn and scuffed as David's—hardly surprising as she had only recently taken up fell-walking.

They each put on their backpacks, which contained extra waterproofs and their emergency medical equipment. Reaching into the back of the car, David picked up his protective helmet, the one he'd been wearing when Kate had first set eyes on him at the surgery when he'd been on his way to another mountain rescue.

He buckled the strap under his chin, then reaching into the car again and brought out another helmet.

'Here. You'd better wear this,' he said, handing the hard plastic helmet to her. 'It's my spare one. I don't want to feel responsible for any head injuries if you slip on the scree or fall down a gully.'

Kate took the helmet and put it on. It had obviously been worn by David in the recent past—in the inside padding lingered a sensual hint of the masculine scent of his hair. Kate strapped it on, her blonde hair sticking out over her jacket collar.

'Suits you,' David said as they walked across the car park to join a similarly attired group of people. There were six of them, and as they approached, a young man of Kate's age greeted them.

'Hi, Doc. Glad you could make it.'

'Gareth, I'd like you to meet my new temporary partner at the practice, Dr Kate Marshall.' David did the introductions. 'Kate, this is Gareth, the team leader.'

There was a printed sticker on Gareth's helmet with the words SUPPORT MOUNTAIN RESCUE. GET LOST! It made Kate smile.

A warm hand clasped hers and bright, dancing eyes smiled out of a suntanned face. 'It's great to meet you, Kate. Welcome to the team. The more, the merrier,' said Gareth with infectious enthusiasm. 'Now, down to business. There's a bloke lost and injured somewhere up there.' He made an expansive gesture, taking in the whole mountain range.

'Don't we have a more specific location?' said David with concern. 'I mean, it's a big place out there.'

'From what his mate told us, we've deduced he must be somewhere around Highfield Crag. Two students decided that it was such a nice day yesterday they'd go out for a stroll on the fells. No proper clothing, no spare food. No map, no compass. They'd gone out in jeans and trainers, can you believe it? Well, yes, I can,' he said, answering his own rhetorical question. 'The number of people who go out walking in jeans and trainers in the high fells, just as though they were going for a gentle walk in the park! Of course, when the mist comes down they're in big trouble. Stuck up a mountain without a map or compass—or even a whistle to give a distress signal.'

Gareth shrugged. 'It's lucky for them there are still mugs like us who'll turn out and look for them.'

'Oh, come on, Gareth,' David said. 'The rescues aren't always like that. Even sensible, well-garbed people can slip or twist an ankle and need help. That's surely one of the reasons we do it, and risk our own lives in the process. These mountains are very unforgiving places. One day that person stuck up there could be one of us.'

'I guess so,' admitted Gareth. He looked at Kate with interest in his eyes. 'Mustn't give our new doctor the impression we're a load of whingers. It's just that when an avoidable emergency like this comes up, well, it gets me more than a little cross.'

Gareth introduced Kate to the others. It was agreed they would split into two search parties, each group taking a doctor with them. Kate was assigned to Gareth's group, and David went with a team led by an attractive dark-haired woman called Maria.

Each team set off, following different mountain paths. Rain was beginning to fall in a persistent drizzle. Kate was walking immediately behind Gareth who shouted out to her over the wind, 'We'd better find him soon. In these conditions, without a bivvy bag or any protective gear, he'll probably be suffering from hypothermia as well as a broken ankle.'

'What's a bivvy bag?' asked Kate, new to fell-walking terminology.

'A waterproof sack. Like a large bin bag, really,' answered Gareth. 'Something every hillwalker should take with them. It's somewhere you can crawl into and keep dry and preserve body temperature if you're benighted—stuck out on the mountains overnight. It only takes up a tiny space in a rucksack but it can be a lifesaver.'

Kate liked Gareth. His warm Northern friendliness made her feel valued and part of the team, even though it was obvious she was a novice when it came to hillwalking.

Gareth kept looking back to make sure his pace wasn't too quick for Kate. 'Let me know if you're having difficulty keeping up,' he said. 'You're much too valuable to lose, Doc.'

His words spurred her on, and she strode up the mountain track with renewed vigour, even though it was getting steeper and harder with every step.

After half a mile or so Gareth spread out his team in what he called a 'critical separation search pattern'. It reminded Kate of the pictures of lines of policemen proceeding shoulder to shoulder in orderly fashion across fields, searching for clues or bodies. Gareth explained to her that their mountain rescue team did it more scientifically, spacing searchers according to a formula based on the average distance at which an object, such as a rucksack or a body, disappears from view in different terrains and under different conditions of visibility.

They had been searching for about half an hour, the two teams keeping in touch with each other through their radio phones. The higher they climbed the stronger the wind and rain became, and the worse the visibility. Gareth was using a flashlight in the vain hope the student might see it. 'If he's still conscious,' said Gareth, more in hope than belief, as they struggled up the boulder strewn mountainside, now even more treacherous and slippery after the morning's icy rain.

They eventually found the student, barely conscious, huddled behind a rock, his eyes glazed, his expression abstracted. Cold and hunger had pushed him into a perilously disorientated state, where he could easily have fallen into one of the many ravines that fractured the mountain.

He was soaking wet and on the point of losing consciousness.

Gareth contacted Maria, the other team leader, on his radio phone. 'We've located him near Clayhithe Gully. Over.'

Kate immediately went to the student to ascertain his medical condition. Other members of the team sank to their knees, opening up their rucksacks and pulling out an impressive array of survival aids and paramedical equipment.

'His name's Richard,' Gareth told Kate as she pulled off her rucksack and knelt beside the youth.

'Hello, Richard,' she said in a calm voice. 'My name's Kate. I'm a doctor. We'll soon have you safely off the mountain. Do you hurt anywhere?'

Huddled up against a rock, which barely gave him any weather protection, Richard looked a sorry sight. He was barely conscious and shivering convulsively. Slowly he moved his head towards Kate.

'Can you hear me, Richard?'

He nodded. Confused eyes peered at her through the rain.

'Do you hurt anywhere?' she repeated.

His lips moved slowly as he whispered: 'My ankle. Can't move it.'

'Which one?'

'Right ankle.'

Kate fumbled with the wet laces on his muddy trainer, finally managing to get it off. She removed his sock and felt gingerly round the swollen ankle. Richard yelped in pain.

'Looks like his mate was right,' said Kate to Gareth. 'Broken ankle it is. We're not going to be able to walk him down with us. He won't be able to put any weight on it.'

'I'll call the helicopter,' said Gareth, squatting down beside her out of the wind.

Kate pulled her medical bag from her rucksack and took out a hypodermic, filling it with ten milligrams of morphine.

'This'll take the pain away, Richard.'

In the meantime, another member of the team, Jane, had draped a buffalo jacket, which looked like an outsize sleeping bag, round him. Kate bandaged his ankle, dressing it as best she could in the circumstances.

A team member named Jake handed Kate an instrument. 'Here's an oximeter, Doc. It attaches to this printout machine. We've just bought it with mountain rescue funds,' Jake added proudly.

'Great,' said Kate, fixing the device to the student's finger. 'Richard, this'll give us a printout of your heart rhythm, blood pressure, pulse and temperature, which will be helpful to the hospital when we get you there.' Kate was talking to the young man constantly, testing his level of consciousness and keeping him awake. It would be so easy, even now, for him to slip into a coma through hypothermia.

The morphine had taken effect, making the pain subside, but Richard was still very cold.

'Can we give him a hot drink?' asked Jane. Kate thought for a moment, then shook her head.

'Best not to give him anything by mouth. He may need an anaesthetic at the hospital to reset the bones in his ankle. Can we warm him up any other way?'

Gareth jumped up, calling all the team members together. 'Right, everyone, shelter time.' With admirable speed and efficiency, Jake, Jane and Gareth erected a windproof nylon casualty shelter round Richard. It was a kind of tent without poles or pegs and all of them, including Kate piled inside it. The idea was for their body heat to raise the air temperature around Richard.

Gareth then turned the shelter into a mountainside Turkish bath by lighting what looked to Kate like an aluminium hookah. A face mask was put over Richard's face. Once the device was working properly, he was breathing in draughts of steamy air through a rubber tube connecting the hookah to his mask.

While all this was going on, Kate was consulting the oximeter, monitoring his vital functions.

'Is his heart all right?' asked Jane, 'because, if there's any problem, we've got a portable defibrillator.'

'I'm impressed,' said Kate. 'This mountain rescue

is better equipped than some hospitals I've known,' she joked. 'Fingers crossed, his heart rate is fine, but obviously there's always an outside chance of cardiac failure with a case like this.'

By now the other team had arrived, led by the striking-looking Maria, closely followed by David. The two teams joined together, piling into the wind shelter with the sole purpose of raising Richard's body temperature.

David moved close to Kate. 'So, you got to him first.' He sounded rather miffed. 'Everything under control?'

'Think so,' Kate said. 'Thanks to all their teamwork and brilliant survival equipment.'

After an hour of the warming treatment Richard's core temperature had been raised by a crucial three degrees. As they waited for the air ambulance to arrive Richard felt well enough to crack a few jokes. He was also feeling very embarrassed about his situation.

'I feel really awful about all the fuss I've caused,' he said apologetically.

'Don't worry,' said Gareth. 'We'll send you the bill later.'

'How much has all this cost?' Richard asked, realising for the first time that there was a price to pay for his foolishness.

'Now, let me see,' said Gareth, pretending to do a complicated mental arithmetic sum. 'There's eight of us here, all highly skilled individuals. Two teachers, an electrician, an engineer, a plumber—top rates of pay for all of them, I'm afraid—plus two doctors. Me, I'm a solicitor and, as you know, you don't get many of them to the pound. Then there's the air ambulance. Let's say, Richard, you'll be having to take out a very large student loan next year.'

Richard looked horrified.

'Fortunately for you we're all volunteers,' said Jane gently, 'but the base costs £15,000 a year to run and to buy the specialist equipment like we're using on you now.'

'All contributions gratefully received,' said Maria, who Kate noticed, was standing pressed up very close to David. In fact, she was pressed up so close to David that he was forced to put his arm around her. On second thoughts, concluded Kate acidly, 'forced' is probably the wrong word. He looks pretty happy about it if you ask me.

Maria seemed to be snuggling her face up to David's whenever she had the opportunity. Over the sound of the howling wind, Kate could make out the odd snatch of conversation between them. She caught some of Maria's words, 'Next week… Is Wednesday OK?'

David replied in the affirmative.

Richard had really perked up now and looked around at the team. He was so relieved at that moment he would probably have given his last penny to the mountain rescue funds. 'Is there anything I can do to help? Anything at all?'

'Just keep off the mountains until you're better prepared,' said Gareth seriously but not unkindly. 'Unless you're wearing the correct gear and with a map and compass. Even on a summer's day the good weather can turn bad, and getting cold and wet can be more than just an uncomfortable inconvenience. It could cost you your life.'

Gareth received a call on his radio phone saying that the helicopter was on its way and needed specific landing instructions. He directed the crew to a valley area below where they now were.

They strapped Richard onto a stretcher and six of them, including Kate and David, carried it between them. The other two members of the team went on ahead to find safe pathways down. At some of the steeper areas they had to tie safety ropes round the stretcher and lower it over the most awkward bolder-strewn slopes.

As they got lower down the mountain and below cloud level, where the ground flattened out into a plateau, they heard the comforting sound of helicopter blades and the locust-like shape hovered into view. The helicopter touched down and David took over the care of the casualty in his role as official team doctor.

'Maria and I will go with him to the hospital,' he told Kate. 'Would you take my car back to the surgery and hold the fort with Gordon till I get back? I'll take a taxi from the hospital, but it could be another hour or so before I'm back at the practice.' He handed Kate his car keys.

'I'd forgotten all about the practice!' said Kate in horror. 'I have a clinic first thing this morning. Gordon will be wondering where I am!'

'No, he won't,' shouted David over the sound of the helicopter blades. 'I phoned him earlier on the mobile and warned him we might be a little late. But it's only seven o'clock now so you'll probably be back in good time.'

Kate was surprised that it was still so early in the morning, just about the time her alarm would be going off. She felt as if she'd already spent a good half-day up and about, so thoroughly absorbed had she been in the drama of the rescue.

Richard was stretchered into the helicopter, closely followed by David and Maria. It took off, leaving the rest of the rescue team to make their way back down the mountain.

'This bit always seems such an anticlimax,' said Gareth as he and Kate walked back down the mountain path together.

'I feel thoroughly drained,' admitted Kate. 'I hope my patients will make allowances for me this morning.'

'Don't let David hear you say that,' joked Gareth. 'He always makes a point of telling us his mountain rescue duties don't interfere with his medical practice. You know how macho he can be!'

'You know David well, do you?' asked Kate.

'Only through the mountain rescue. He's a good bloke, and a great doctor.' Gareth looked at Kate, admiration in his eyes. 'Just like you are. Cool and calm under fire. Inspiring confidence!'

'I didn't do anything really,' said Kate modestly. 'Nothing special, anyway.'

'Don't you believe it. You'd be surprised what a difference it makes to team morale to have a proper doctor along—not just one of us with vague paramedic training.' He smiled at her. 'And you've got a great bedside manner, or should I say hillside manner?'

Kate smiled back at him. The rain had now stopped and the sun was just peeping out from behind a cloud.

'How many rescues a year are you called out on, Gareth?'

'About fifty.'

'Phew,' whistled Kate. 'Talking of a good hillside manner, I thought you were very restrained just now in your words to that foolish young man. I was expecting you to give him a right old tongue-lashing after what you said in the car park earlier!'

'Good heavens, no,' Gareth replied. 'Our job is to find them, care for them and get them down. The ticking-off comes later. Never on the hillside.'

The car park came into view and the team went off in various directions towards their own cars, saying cheery goodbyes to each other. Gareth was still walking next to Kate.

'Are you all right for a lift home?' he asked.

'I'm driving David's car back, thanks,' she said.

Gareth seemed reluctant to get into his car and lingered a while, before opening the door. 'Kate,' he said casually, 'fancy coming out for a drink one night?'

He saw the look of hesitation in her eyes.

'Only because you're officially on the team now, of course,' he added. 'It's an old mountain rescue tradition. The team leader buys each new member a welcoming drink.' He grinned at her as he unbuckled his helmet and took it off, revealing a head of short-cropped fair hair. He was a good-looking man, thought Kate, and, though not as tall or as handsome as David, he nevertheless was a man who would have no trouble attracting women.

'I'd love a drink with my team leader,' replied Kate, in the same light-hearted vein. 'Far be it for me to break with tradition.'

'Tonight suit you?' he asked, pushing home his advantage. 'That's part of the tradition. It has to be the same evening as the rescue or it's a hundred years' bad luck.'

'Tonight will be fine,' said Kate, laughing, 'but I must warn you I'll be wanting an early night in bed.'

'You really are very forward, Dr Marshall! Trying to lead an innocent young solicitor astray.' He grinned impishly. 'Pick you up at eight.'

By the time Kate had got back to the practice, showered and changed into her 'doctor' clothes, it was still only nine o'clock. She met Gordon as they were each walking into their consulting rooms.

'Didn't expect to find you here,' he said. 'I thought you and David were clinging to a rock face. He certainly gave me that impression when he very kindly rang me at 6 a.m. this morning.'

'Sorry if we woke you up, Gordon,' said Kate. 'David went with the casualty to the hospital. I've no idea when he'll be back.'

'Talk of the devil,' said Gordon, as David, in his mountain gear, walked in.

Kate's morning clinic seemed to take much longer than usual. She realised it was because she'd been up since the crack of dawn, and by the time the lunch-break came along she had been up for nearly eight hours and was absolutely starving.

As she walked away from her desk David popped his head round the door and stepped in.

'Wondered if you were going to the Hare and Hounds for a butty?' he asked. 'Thought we might go together. We've got some unfinished business to discuss.' He looked deadly serious. Kate was in no doubt about which bit of unfinished business he was referring to. David wanted to tell her all about Julia—and probably to once again call her father a liar.

Kate was in no mood for such a highly charged emotional discussion, certainly not in the middle of her working day.

'Well, actually,' said Kate evasively, 'I thought I'd go up to the flat and cook myself something for lunch.'

David raised his eyebrows. 'A cooked lunch? What's brought all this on?'

'I didn't have time for breakfast, that's all, and it seems hours since I had a proper meal.'

David made a point of checking his watch. 'Fifteen hours, actually,' he said.

Kate looked puzzled.

'At Danilo's,' he prompted. 'Remember? Surely your memory's not that bad.'

Kate's hand flew to her mouth. 'Oh, yes. I'd forgotten for a moment. So much has happened since then, with the rescue and everything. Danilo's seems ages ago.'

'I hope you've not forgotten *everything*,' he said

quietly. 'Everything that happened before we got that most inconvenient phone call from Gareth.'

Kate began to feel uncomfortable, a prickly feeling invading her armpits. He's doing it again, she thought behind gritted teeth. Trying to exert his will over me, pull me into his web. Take up where he left off.

She'd fallen for it last night, after drinking a little too much wine, but this time she was stone cold sober. She wasn't going to make the same mistake twice.

'Anyway,' she continued, pretending she didn't know what he was alluding to, 'I'm going out for a drink tonight. I don't want to spend all my time in pubs. People will think I'm an alcoholic.'

'You're going out tonight?' He was visibly taken aback. 'Alone?'

'No,' she replied airily. 'As a matter of fact, I'm going out with Gareth.'

'Gareth from the mountain rescue?'

'Well, I don't know any other men called Gareth around here!'

David was incredulous. 'Why on earth are you going out with Gareth?'

Kate picked up her handbag and tried to get through the door, only David was blocking her path. She looked him in the eye. He really was very put out by her revelation.

'I'm going out with Gareth because he asked me.' Kate began to feel annoyed at David's cross-examination. 'Now, if you'll excuse me, David, I'd like to go and get something to eat.'

He didn't move. His hand was on the doorknob, preventing her exit.

'Gareth just used the rescue as an opportunity to chat you up—'

'Well, I noticed you weren't averse to doing some chatting up yourself on the mountain rescue.'

'What on earth are you talking about?' he stormed.

'Don't look so innocent, David Firth. I saw you with that Maria woman. She was all over you, and you didn't seem to object one tiny bit. I heard you fixing up to meet her next week. And I noticed you made damn sure it was just the two of you going back on the helicopter.'

He stiffened defensively. 'Don't be ridiculous! Maria's a married woman.'

'That's never stopped you in the past, has it? In fact, it seems to add to the attraction where you're concerned!'

Seeing her way now clear, she grabbed the door-knob and tried to open the door quickly. David slammed his foot against it, barring her way.

'And what the hell do you mean by that?' He spoke in a low, threatening voice, his face stiff and white with anger.

'I know all about you,' she retorted vehemently. 'Julia. She was a married woman and that didn't stop you, did it?'

'I've told you, it was all a terrible misunderstanding where Julia was concerned,' he protested.

'I'll bet it was!' sniped Kate. 'Is it always a "misunderstanding" when a woman doesn't instantly let you take her to bed?'

'You know, Kate, you can be quite a little bitch.' His eyes bored into her, blazing with anger.

'The truth hurts, doesn't it, David? Admit it. When you don't get your own way with a woman, you just force yourself on her.'

Instead of inflaming his anger, this last accusation seemed to calm David down. He didn't answer for a beat, and when he did his voice was quiet and controlled.

'I don't recall having to do much forcing with you last night. You wanted me as much as I wanted you. And if the mountain rescue hadn't intervened we would have made love. We *both* knew that. We *both* wanted to.'

The reminder of her foolish behaviour the previous night made Kate see red.

'Well, I've changed my mind. I want nothing more to do with you—on a personal basis that is. From now on we're going to keep our relationship purely professional.'

He remained rooted to the spot, his foot still firmly wedged in the door.

'If you don't move away from my door this instant,' she snarled at him, 'I will scream so loudly you'll go temporarily deaf in one, if not both ears.'

She saw his hand clench, the knuckles showing white. For a split second she was afraid he might actually hit her. Then he took a deep breath. The tension between them relaxed and he moved away from the door, letting her through.

But the cold, deadly stare he gave her shrivelled any moment of triumph she might have temporarily enjoyed.

CHAPTER SEVEN

WHY on earth, Kate asked herself, was she standing outside in the surgery car park, all dressed and ready to go, a good five minutes before she was due to be picked up?

Could it be that she just couldn't bear the thought of Gareth bumping into David if she let him come to the house and ring the doorbell?

Guilty feelings welled up in Kate's mind. Come to think of it, why on earth was she going out for a drink with Gareth in the first place? She must surely have realised it could cause trouble between the two men, especially as they had to work together on the mountain rescue team.

To hell with David and his sensitivities, she decided as she saw Gareth's car arrive. Giving Gareth a winning smile, she slipped into the passenger seat next to him.

'You look smashing,' he said, casting an admiring eye over her outfit—white silk shirt and short denim skirt—the same clothes she'd worn the day she'd arrived at the practice. Her hair was gleaming and her eyes shone.

'I'm relieved you're in denim, too,' she remarked, seeing his jeans and check shirt. 'I wasn't sure how posh a place we were going to for this "traditional" drink. Being a solicitor, I thought you might turn up in a suit and then I'd have felt terribly under-dressed.'

'I wear suits all day in the office,' Gareth replied, turning the car round and driving back onto the road. 'Consequently, it takes an awful lot of persuading to get me to put on a suit in the evening as well.'

They drove past the Hare and Hounds and Kate gave an inward sigh of relief. She didn't like the idea of being with Gareth in her local pub, just in case David also decided he would pop in there for a drink. Damn, she thought, why can't I have just one evening when I don't think about David all the time? Gritting her teeth, she made a determined effort to banish him from her mind.

The pub Gareth took her to was up in the mountains, with a glorious view over the countryside and lake. As they walked in, he stooped under the low beam over the entrance where a sign warned, 'Duck or grouse.'

'What a great pub,' said Kate as they entered the cosy bar.

'My favourite,' Gareth said. 'Not too scruffy, but not tarted up by some big brewery taking away its individual character. No fairy lights round the bar, no large-screen telly, no piped music. And the best real ale for miles around. Bliss!'

Kate sat at a small corner table while Gareth brought their drinks over.

'Peanuts? Pork scratchings? Elephants' toenails?' he enquired of her.

'No, thanks,' said Kate with a laugh, sipping her cool wine. 'This'll do nicely.'

He slid into the seat next to her. They chatted in

an easy, friendly way, and before long Kate was beginning to enjoy his company thoroughly. He told her about his work and how he and his partner took on a mixed bag of clients.

'We'd like to specialise in seriously rich clients who need lots of top-quality legal advice and who pay their bills on time. What we tend to get are the seriously poor, desperately deserving clients whose cases take up enormous amounts of time and whose bills have to be kept to the minimum. Even then, we're lucky to get paid.'

'My heart bleeds for you,' said Kate with a twinkle in her eyes. 'Just don't go telling your sob stories to any junior hospital doctor who's been on call for twenty-four hours. That's the kind of regime I save my sympathy for, having been there myself not all that long ago.'

Over a second drink, Gareth told Kate about the mountain rescue—some of their triumphs, some of their tragedies. 'It's not all good news like today. Sometimes we don't get there in time.' He asked Kate how experienced a fell-walker she was.

'Not very,' she admitted. 'I joined a local group when I first arrived, but I've only been out with them a couple of times, on very easy rambles. I would have thought my inexperience was patently obvious on the rescue today.'

'Not at all,' he said gallantly, a look of admiration returning to his eyes. 'You were magnificent. Kept up a good pace. Didn't collapse in a heap at the first steep climb. Then turned into a ministering angel with cool efficiency.'

There was a silence between them, and for a moment she thought he was going to kiss her. Instead, he cleared his throat and looked into his beer.

'Would you like to come hillwalking with me one day?' he ventured.

He was making a pass at her, Kate realised, and not for the first time that evening. It was obvious to her he wanted more than friendship.

But did she? If she wasn't prepared to get into a relationship with Gareth, shouldn't she nip it in the bud before anyone got hurt?

So why did she smile encouragingly at him, saying, 'Yes, Gareth, I'd like that very much.' Was it because she enjoyed playing with fire? Or was it because she hoped against hope that, by encouraging Gareth, she might be able to wean herself off the fatal attraction she felt for David? Was she hoping she could cure herself of dependency on a dangerous drug—which is what David had become to her?

'Terrific,' he said. 'How about tomorrow, Saturday? The weather forecast is good and I'll plan a route that isn't too strenuous.'

'Why not?' agreed Kate.

Downing his pint, he stood up. 'We'd better get that early night, Dr Marshall.'

They strolled back to the car through the pleasant coolness of the evening air. He slipped an arm round Kate's shoulders, and as they entered the shadow of a tree he pulled her to him and kissed her.

She closed her eyes and let herself be carried away on the sensation. But it was not a kiss of which dreams were made. It was like kissing...well, just anyone. Nothing special, nothing memorable. Nothing to make her want more.

As they pulled away and walked back to the car, Kate felt tears sting her eyes. She hadn't realised how much she had wanted Gareth's kiss to be magical, to feel so good it would send those thrilling darts of pleasure through her body. She hadn't realised just how desperately she had wanted him to make her respond to his touch the way David could.

A great sadness descended on her as she resigned herself to the fact that Gareth, even though he was an attractive and thoroughly nice man, wasn't the one to awaken in her the primitive beat of hot desire.

Only one man had ever done that. David Firth. And though she could dream about him—fantasise about him—never, ever could she surrender to him. That would be like surrendering her soul to the devil.

They'd agreed on an early start—but not too early. Kate had made herself a packed lunch and filled a flask with coffee.

'So, that's lunch, hot drink, map, whistle, compass, waterproofs, spare sweater and socks.' She said her check-list out loud, packing everything neatly into her rucksack before leaving her flat.

Like the previous night, Kate was waiting in the car park when Gareth arrived. Once again she didn't want to risk an awkward confrontation with David.

Gareth jumped out of his car and loaded her rucksack in the boot alongside his own.

He pulled a sheet of paper out of his pocket. 'Here,' he said, handing it to her. 'Stick this on your door. It says where we're going, the route we're taking and when we expect to be back. That's rule one of hillwalking. Always let someone know how to find you in case you don't turn up.'

Kate ran back inside quickly and was just pinning the note on her door when, to her dismay, she heard David's feet on the stairs.

'Going walking?' he said, glancing at her boots and clothing.

'Yes,' she said, avoiding looking at him.

'On your own?'

'With Gareth, actually.' Embarrassment possessed her and she felt colour rising in her cheeks.

'My goodness, you don't waste time, do you?' he said bitingly.

She tried to keep the nervousness out of her voice as she spoke in staccato bursts. 'Gareth asked me. And I thought I'd go.'

The second's silence between them seemed like an hour.

He drew a breath. 'I see,' he said derisively, turning his back on her and walking away. As she ran down the stairs, she heard his flat door slam shut.

Gareth drove them out of the car park, fired with enthusiasm for the day ahead. 'I feel great!' he said, clasping the steering-wheel. 'I feel like this every time I get out my walking boots. Something deep and primeval inside me makes me want to get out there and get up the mountains!'

His enthusiasm was infectious and soon Kate began to relax after her unpleasant confrontation with David.

'So, where are you taking me, Mr Team Leader?'

'We're going up High Street,' he replied.

'High Street? I thought we were going up a mountain, not shopping.'

Gareth laughed. 'High Street is a mountain or, to be more correct, a footpath on a mountain ridge. A long whale-backed crest, high in the fells. It's actually an ancient Roman road, trodden through the ages by a whole variety of different travellers—marching Roman soldiers, marauding brigands, local shepherds and, nowadays, by people like us, walking for pleasure.

'It goes through some very high land, linking a whole line of peaks. The reason I've chosen it for us today is that the walking is relatively easy, a nice grassy path with some good views of Ullswater and other smaller lakes. Plus the fact that all the climbing involved will be done at the beginning of the walk when we're relatively fresh, leaving us with nice plateau walking through the day and downhill walking at the end when we're knackered!'

'Sounds brilliant,' said Kate. 'You seem to have planned it very well.'

'That's the secret of successful hillwalking. Knowing exactly the lie of the terrain and not leaving the difficult bits to the end when you're tired.'

He slipped his hand from the steering-wheel and sought hers, giving it a squeeze. 'I don't want to put you off hillwalking by taking you on a really tough walk this first time.'

His tone made Kate feel slightly uneasy. Gareth seemed to be jumping to conclusions, she thought with dismay. He seemed to be assuming they would be going out on many more hillwalks in the future. She resolved to tackle the subject with him when the time was appropriate. She could not let him go on thinking their relationship could develop into something more meaningful. She at least owed him that much.

They drove into Patterdale, a small village on the edge of Ullswater. Kate was struck by the number of walkers around the place. There was a distinctly alpine atmosphere about the village, with its huddle of pretty houses and shops, nestling in a green and wooded valley, surrounded by majestic mountains.

'That's Helvellyn,' said Gareth, pointing to the tallest of the mountain ranges. 'It's a magnificent, dramatic mountain—and a great walk. But we'll save that for another day.'

Kate swallowed hard. She said nothing.

'Today we're going over there.' Gareth pointed to a mountain range on the other side of Ullswater.

'And I suppose we're going to swim to get to it,' joked Kate.

'Only if the boat sinks. I'm starting you off gently, with a sedate ferry ride across to Howtown. That's where we'll start walking.'

Gareth parked the car in an official car park, next to several others. They put on their rucksacks and followed a group of other similarly attired walkers who were heading in the direction of the lake.

The ferry had just arrived and about thirty passengers were disembarking.

'I've never been here before,' said Kate, looking across the lake from the landing stage, 'even though I was born and bred in the north of England. I'm quite ashamed to say this is the first time I've set eyes on Ullswater.'

'I think it's probably my favourite lake of all,' said Gareth. 'It was also the favourite lake of that greatest of all mountain writers, the legendary A. Wainwright. He said it won his vote as the fairest of them all, and that Patterdale seems far too good a place for this poor polluted earth. He wrote that when he visualised heaven it wasn't St Peter at the gate and angels sitting on clouds that he saw but a paradise modelled on Patterdale and Ullswater.'

After buying their tickets, Kate and Gareth went on board the ferry. Shortly after, the small boat headed out along the long, narrow lake which curved round to the right, its full length hidden from view.

'This ferry goes to Pooley Bridge at the far end of Ullswater,' explained Gareth, standing by the railing with Kate as they looked out onto the beautiful waters of the lake. 'We're getting off at Howtown, about halfway along.'

They fell silent, standing by the rail, just admiring the view and listening to the throbbing of the engine. Gareth put his hand round Kate's waist and pulled her close to him. She tensed, making him aware of her resistance.

'What's the matter?' he asked as she pulled away from him. 'Gone off me already?'

Kate turned to face him. She spoke firmly but gently. 'No, I haven't gone off you, Gareth. I like you very much. As a friend.'

He looked crestfallen. 'I was hoping we could be more than just friends, Kate.'

She picked her words carefully. 'I don't think that's possible, Gareth. It's nothing to do with you.

It's me… I'm not ready for a more serious relationship yet.'

He turned away, looking out over the lake. After a minute or so he turned back. His face registered disappointment. 'Well, I can always live in hope, I suppose.' He smiled ruefully. He was trying very hard to hide his true feelings.

Kate felt as miserable as she knew he must be, but managed to return a bright smile.

After about twenty minutes the ferry reached the small landing stage at Howtown, a tiny hamlet on the other side of Ullswater. As they were preparing to get off the boat, Kate saw a familiar figure standing a few yards off the shore. It was David, and he was leaning against his car, obviously waiting for them to step off the ferry.

Kate felt rage rising in her throat. How dared he follow her? The man was a maniac, hounding her every movement. He was behaving insanely. Couldn't he take no for an answer? Hadn't she made it perfectly clear that, on a personal level, she wanted nothing more to do with him?

Gareth also noticed David standing there and pointed him out to Kate as they walked up the small shingle beach.

'There's David,' he said in a puzzled voice. 'Wonder what he wants?'

'Yes, I wonder,' snarled Kate through clenched teeth.

As they walked towards him, David stood upright and moved in Kate's direction. His face looked grim. Something about him sent a shock of fear through her.

'What is it?' she asked, cold striking deep into her heart.

David put his hand on her arm. 'Kate, it's your father. He's been taken ill. He collapsed during a lecture yesterday. They're not sure what the matter is, but he's been taken to hospital.'

'Oh, my God,' said Kate, feeling her legs give way. David held her with both hands, supporting her against his body.

'The message came shortly after you'd left. Fortunately I was able to work out where you'd be from the note on your door. I arrived in Patterdale just as the ferry had left so I drove round the lake and here I am.'

'I must go to him straight away,' said Kate, regaining the strength in her legs. 'Will you give me a lift back to the surgery so I can drive over to Cheshire?'

'I'll do better than that,' said David. 'I'll drive you there myself. You're in no fit state to take on two hours' driving after receiving a shock like that.'

'But I need to pick up some things in case I have to stay over,' protested Kate, distractedly.

'I've already done that for you,' said David, indicating a bag on the back seat of the car. 'I put some stuff in an overnight bag—knickers, nightie, toothbrush, that sort of thing.'

Kate drew in her breath, taken aback by his efficiency. 'How did you get into my flat? It was locked.' It was all she could think of saying.

'There's a spare set of keys in Reception,' he replied.

'Why don't you and David get off straight away?' said Gareth gently.

Since she'd received the bad news of her father, Kate had completely forgotten about Gareth, who was standing a few feet away, not wanting to interrupt or intrude.

'Oh, Gareth, I'd completely forgotten about our walk,' said Kate in confusion, still trying to take in the implications of her father's collapse. 'I'm so sorry to have messed things up for you. What will you do now?'

'Silly girl, don't worry about me. I'll go up the mountain just like I was going to do,' he said, touching her tentatively on the arm. 'Just get going as quickly as you can.' He kissed her warmly on the cheek. 'And when you get there I hope the news is good.' He walked towards the footpath, saying to David as he passed, 'Take care of her, David.'

They both stared after him as he hitched his rucksack securely on his shoulders and disappeared from view into a wooded lane.

David looked curiously at Kate, searching her face for any clue to the relationship between her and Gareth. She knew what must be going through his mind—he was wondering whether she was now Gareth's girlfriend. It was an assumption that any onlooker might make, judging by the familiar way he'd kissed her, openly and without embarrassment, right in front of David. His instruction to David to take care of her only added to the assumption, implying some sort of proprietorial interest, some personal claim on her.

Kate, of course, knew this wasn't what Gareth had intended.

But David wasn't to know that. Judging by the annoyed look on his face as he took her rucksack from her, he had jumped to some very wrong conclusions.

They set off, driving by the side of Ullswater, through the town of Pooley Bridge, heading in the direction of the M6 motorway.

Kate sat grim-faced, tense with anxiety about her father. 'Did they give any more details about how he collapsed, or what tests they're doing?'

'No,' replied David, driving at the maximum speed permitted. 'Why don't you lie back and relax? The seat control is at the side. There's nothing you can do right now and worrying about it won't help. And, before you ask, I do know the way to the hospital, thank you—I checked it on the map, before setting out.'

He switched on the car radio and selected a classical music station. Kate spent the rest of the journey listening to the soothing music, trying to put all anxious thoughts out of her head.

It was late morning when they pulled into the hospital car park. Before getting out, she turned to David. 'Would you mind not coming in to see my father?' she said hesitantly. 'You see, he doesn't know I'm working with you...with all that thing about Julia and—'

'I understand,' interrupted David. 'You needn't worry, I won't do anything to upset him in his present condition. And if meeting me again would upset him, then I'll keep well out of the way.'

Kate was touched by his sensitivity. 'I'm sorry it has to be like this,' she said, swallowing hard, 'after you've driven me here and everything. It's just that if he recognises you—' As she spoke she was struck by a frightening thought. 'That's assuming he's conscious. He may not be. He may not even recognise me. I have a terrible premonition there's something dreadfully wrong with him.' Kate broke down.

David put a comforting arm around her, stroking her soothingly. 'There's no point in getting upset until you know what's happened, and until you know the prognosis. Face that hurdle when you come it.'

His words made good sense. Kate pulled herself up straight, dabbing her eyes with the large handkerchief he gave her. As she opened the car door David said, 'Kate?'

She turned and looked at him.

'Whatever happens, just remember I'll be waiting here for you,' he said.

She nodded, touched by his words and touched by the fact he seemed to know just the right thing to say to give her the courage to face up to whatever lay ahead. An hour later, Kate asked David to come into the hospital waiting area. She desperately needed his advice and support. Vital decisions had to be made and she didn't want to make them on her own.

Kate had been shocked at her father's appearance when she'd seen him lying in his hospital bed. He'd been in a small room, in a semi-conscious state, attached to various monitoring and intravenous devices.

The nurse who had taken Kate in to him had explained that her father had collapsed and fallen to the floor while giving a lecture to a hall full of medical students. They were doing tests to find out what the cause of his collapse might have been. He had recovered consciousness but hadn't been fully attentive. He'd been so groggy Kate hadn't even been sure if he'd known where he was, or that she was there.

Kate had insisted on speaking to the consultant in charge of her father. 'I'm a doctor,' she'd told the nurse, hoping that would have had some influence on how quickly she got to see the top man. Normally Kate would have been reluctant to pull strings in this way, but where her own father was concerned she'd been darned if she'd let anything stand in her way.

The specialist had been bleeped and after what had seemed an age he'd walked into Dr Marshall's room.

'As you're a doctor yourself,' he said, 'I'll dispense with the bedside manner stuff and give you the facts straight. Or at least as straight as I can.'

The consultant picked up a chart at the foot of Dr Marshall's bed. 'Your father may have had a stroke, or he may have a brain tumour. Until we do a CT scan we won't know which it is. As your father is not properly conscious and able to speak coherently, he has been unable to give us any symptoms or any clue as to which of the diagnoses it could be. As you know, the signs of certain brain tumours and stroke are very similar.'

Kate felt as if she'd been struck with a blunt object. Brain tumour or stroke? Either one was a terrible blow.

'He's been having a lot of headaches recently,' she said quietly. 'And he's also been experiencing double vision.' Even before the consultant replied, Kate had formed the words in her own mind. The words 'brain tumour'.

It was at that moment she felt a desperate need for David to be by her side. Kate called him in from the car park and told him her suspicions. The hospital consultant suggested they all sit down in his office to discuss the case.

'We're sending your father for a scan this afternoon and then we'll have the diagnosis confirmed,' he said. 'But after what you've told me...' he turned to Kate '...it looks very likely that a brain tumour is the culprit. If that is the case, we shall have to move him to another hospital as we don't have the facilities or the specialist surgeon to do the operation. Presuming, of course, that the tumour is operable.'

Kate's hands began to shake. 'You think it might be inoperable?' she said with despair in her voice.

David slipped his hand round hers, enclosing it in a warm, comforting grasp. 'Let's not jump to conclusions,' he said firmly. 'I suggest we take it one step at a time.' He faced the consultant. 'When will we get the CT results?' he asked.

'Later on this afternoon,' he answered, rising from his desk. 'I'll contact you as soon as possible. In the meantime, we're keeping your father as comfortable and pain-free as possible, and maintaining his hydration with a drip.'

Kate sat with her father until he was taken away for the brain scan, after which she went and joined David in the hospital waiting area. He bought them some coffee and sandwiches from the small canteen area, and even though Kate wasn't hungry she managed to force something down.

'If the scan does confirm it's a tumour,' said David, broaching the subject for the first time since they'd spoken with the consultant, 'I know just the man to deal with it—the best neurosurgeon in the world.'

Kate looked up at him, a glimmer of hope in her eyes. 'You do? What's his name?'

'Mr Roger Firth. My big brother.'

She was astounded. 'Your brother is a neurosurgeon? Where?'

'In Birmingham,' replied David. 'I put a call through to him while you were with your father before they took him for the scan. I spoke to Roger and he's willing to operate on your father. They've also got a surgical bed free at the moment.'

'Oh, that's wonderful!' said Kate, relief in her voice. 'That was going to be my next hurdle, wondering how soon they'd find a hospital bed for him and which part of the country they'd have to send him to. Do you think there'll be any problems with sending him to Birmingham? Won't the consultant mind you pushing in and making decisions over his head?'

'I don't care if he does,' replied David assertively, 'but I should think he'll be very pleased for someone to take a patient off his hands. That man looked one very harassed consultant. He sure as hell won't be fighting me for the privilege of deciding which operating table your father ends up on.'

By early evening, Kate's father was in an emergency ambulance and on his way to Birmingham. The CT scan had confirmed the diagnosis of brain tumour and the hospital consultant had, as David had predicted, been only too happy to let David's brother take over the case. The fact that he was impressed by Roger Firth's medical reputation made things run even smoother.

As they followed in the wake of the ambulance's flashing blue light, Kate asked David if she should let Gordon know that she might be away from the practice for some days.

'I already did,' said David. 'And I told him he may have to manage without me for the next day or so as well. Anyway, tomorrow's Sunday so let's take one day at a time.'

'I feel such a nuisance,' said Kate. 'I'm sure I should have been able to manage on my own, driving down here and dealing with things.'

'I'm sure you could have done it admirably,' agreed David. 'I just wanted to be on hand to do what I could, that's all.'

Kate glanced at him sideways. An unworthy thought occurred to her and she spoke it out loud. 'Thinking you might take advantage of my vulnerability, you mean?' The moment the words were out she regretted having said them. After all, David had been magnificent the way he had rallied round.

Instead of reacting to her stinging remark, he spoke calmly and without rancour. 'It wasn't just for you I did it. I was very concerned for your father. He's someone for whom I once felt great love and respect.'

Dr Marshall was admitted to the surgical ward and a call was put out for Mr Firth, the neurosurgeon.

Roger Firth looked remarkably like his brother,

though not quite so tall. Kate estimated he must be six or seven years older than David.

The two brothers greeted each other genially and David introduced Kate, who handed over her father's medical file and prints of the CT scan.

After studying the scan, Roger asked Kate about any symptoms her father had exhibited in the weeks prior to his collapse.

'He just seemed to be having rather a lot of headaches,' Kate recalled. 'I wasn't too concerned because he's a doctor himself and should have been aware of any serious condition developing.'

'Not necessarily,' said Roger. 'People, even some doctors, tend to assume that the headaches caused by a brain tumour are going to be excruciating. They can be, but the headaches caused by increased intracranial pressure can be very similar to ordinary tension headaches or migraines. Did he have any other symptoms—of a focal nature, for instance?'

'He mentioned he was having trouble with double vision,' Kate said. 'I must say at the time alarm bells rang in my head, but my father just waved aside my concerns, telling me not to fuss, saying he just needed new spectacles.'

'Again, he could have been right, but by then he must have begun to wonder if there was perhaps something more seriously wrong with him.' Roger Firth clipped the X-rays to a light-box on his office wall. 'But you know what doctors are like. We're often worse than non-medics at facing up to the fact that we could be ill. Probably a result of our early medical student days when we were convinced we had every disease in the book once we'd learned about it.'

Roger studied the X-rays for several minutes. Kate could hardly bring herself to ask the question that was uppermost in her mind.

'Is the tumour operable?' she asked almost in a whisper.

'I think so,' said Roger. 'You can see it here, in the cerebellar hemisphere. So far so good—it's much safer there than in the brain stem.' He pointed to a dark area on the X-ray, at the right-hand side of the brain. 'His tumour is this irregular avascular mass in the right parietal lobe.'

'What are his chances?' Kate stared at the horrifying picture of her father's brain.

'We won't know for sure till we do a craniotomy and take a biopsy sample. If it's a large tumour, his chances aren't so good. If, however, this dark mass is made up of cystic material, then his chances are pretty good. If it's a gliotic cyst caused by a small tumour, and we can get all the nodules out, his chances of a full recovery are excellent. But I mustn't raise your hopes too much at this early stage.'

Kate felt sick with apprehension. 'When will you operate?'

'As soon as possible. The pressure in his skull is increasing by the minute. Time is of the essence. They will be prepping him now and my team will probably be scrubbing up as we speak. That's what I must also do right now.' Roger unclipped the X-rays and took them with him.

'Kate and I will wait outside,' David told him.

'Perhaps someone could keep us informed about each stage of the operation?'

'Sure,' said Roger, walking briskly out of the room. 'Follow me. I'll show you where to wait.'

Kate and David sat outside the theatre, as close to the scene of the operation as they could be without actually being in the operating theatre.

'It could be a long wait,' said David. 'Brain surgery can take a very long time. Let's hope it does take a long time.'

Kate looked at him in puzzlement. 'What are you talking about?'

David was grim-faced. 'Just think about it, Kate. If they get inside and find the tumour isn't operable, they'll just close him up again. That takes much less time than doing the intricate surgery involved in removing the tumour. I'm sorry to be saying this, but we both know the score. So, in a way, the longer we wait here, the more hopeful it will be.'

Kate nodded, biting her lip to hold back the tears.

Over the general operating theatre chit-chat, Kate became aware of a rather disturbing sound, like the sound of an electric drill. 'What are they doing now, do you think?' she asked David anxiously.

'Cutting through his skull, I would imagine.'

'Oh, yes, of course,' she said, as all the textbook details of a brain operation came flooding back to her, this time in shocking reality.

An hour into the operation, a nurse came out to speak to them. 'Mr Firth says to tell you things are looking hopeful. The mass is about seventy per cent cystic.'

The relief that swept over Kate made her feel faint. 'Oh, thank God!' That was all she could say.

'We've removed the cystic fluid and located the tumour,' continued the nurse, 'and we've just sent tissue samples to the path. lab to find out whether there's any malignancy present. Now we're just waiting for the biopsy results, before completing the operation.'

'I wanted to tell you the good news myself,' said Roger Firth, 'before I scrubbed up again to complete the operation.'

At the words 'good news' Kate's heart leapt.

'It's as I suspected—a pilocytic astrocytoma, a benign tumour which has been secreting fluid and causing the hydrocephalus as it formed a large cyst. The path. lab analysis confirmed it to be non-malignant. If we can remove the complete nodule from the cyst wall, your father's chances of a full recovery are excellent.'

'That's wonderful news, Roger,' said Kate in relief. 'Thank you so much. I can't tell you how grateful I am.' Tears welled up in her eyes.

David clutched her by the shoulder and she could feel his iron grip, tight and tense. 'That's great news, Roger,' he said, holding his breath momentarily, then exhaling slowly.

'Now that you know the news is good, no doubt you'll feel happier during the waiting.'

Kate's eyes followed Roger as he went back inside.

The scene in the operating theatre was a familiar one—lots of high-tech equipment, long cords and bottles, shiny instrument trays. A huddle of green-garbed people were stooping over the operating table, working under the bright arc lights. Roger and his assistant surgeon both wore head-lights, like miners' lamps.

Roger Firth pulled off his bloodstained latex gloves. The surgery had taken four hours.

'I think we removed all of the tumour and the cystic fluid. The pressure on his brain is now relieved—your father should be back to normal in a couple of weeks' time.'

'What is his prognosis?' asked Kate.

'Good...very good, I would say,' answered Roger. 'Especially as I did the operation.'

'My brother is a great surgeon,' said David, peeling off his theatre greens, 'but his greatest virtue is modesty.'

He ducked just in time to miss the swipe of latex gloves across the back of his head.

CHAPTER EIGHT

STEPPING down from the train three days later, Kate looked around for the taxi she was expecting to be there to meet her. Following the good news about her father's operation, Kate had persuaded David to drive back to the Lakes, leaving her to make her own arrangements.

She had stayed two nights in a small hotel near the hospital, spending the days at her father's bedside. Dr Marshall, as Roger Firth had predicted, was making an excellent recovery and would be well enough to return home in two weeks' time. Kate and her father had discussed what kind of nursing help he would then need and for how long. Although he hated any kind of fuss being made over him, after a good talking-to by the neurosurgeon he'd agreed to accept Kate's offer to spend two weeks at home with him after his discharge from hospital.

In the meantime they'd both decided she might as well return to the Lakes and to her job in the practice. She'd discussed all this over several phone calls with Gordon and David. Between them they had come to an arrangement that she would return on the Tuesday evening and work in the practice for the next ten days during the time her father would still be in hospital. Gordon and David would then book a temporary locum for two weeks while Kate went back to Cheshire to look after her father.

Before catching the train north, she had phoned Tracy and asked her to arrange a taxi as she had been warned she'd be unlikely to find one on spec at the small rural station.

As she walked through the ticket barrier she saw David sprinting towards her. 'Thought I might have misjudged it,' he said breathlessly. 'Got held up with a patient and I'm afraid I cut it a bit fine. Still, the main thing is I made it on time.'

Kate couldn't disguise the fact that she was delighted to see him. She walked towards him in the warm evening sun.

'I thought Tracy was ordering a taxi for me,' she said, returning his welcoming smile.

'And here it is,' he said, pointing to his mud-splattered Range Rover.

'Well, all I can say is, Dr Firth, with such a filthy car I certainly hope you're not expecting a tip.'

They drove back over the hills, towards the setting sun. The road climbed high into the mountains, before dropping down to the valley where their small town nestled. Instead of continuing along the mountain road that led to the practice, David pulled off the road and onto a grassy plateau with a magnificent view of the lake, mountains and setting sun. He cut the engine and gave a deep, sensuous sigh. 'No matter how many times I see it, I never tire of this view—especially at sunset.'

They got out of the car and walked together in the last rays of the sun as it suffused the sky and bathed the mountains in an orange glow.

David put his arm around Kate's shoulder and they stood in silence for several magical moments. Then he kissed her, cupping his hands round her face. All the longing she felt for him surged through her veins. She ached for him.

'I brought you here for a purpose,' he said huskily, holding her trembling body tight against his. He released her from his tight embrace and gazed down at her. His eyes were soft, but his face was serious.

'I want to tell you the whole rotten story,' he said slowly, picking his words with care. 'I want to tell you what happened between me and Julia and your father. I want you to hear the truth. The whole truth. Not just your father's version of it.'

Kate opened her mouth to protest, but David silenced her, placing his fingers on her lips.

'I want you to hear the truth,' he repeated. 'It hurts me that you feel such anger about it, that you're judging me by another man's story. How can there be any trust between us, any future for us, if you won't give me the chance to explain?' There was deep emotion in his voice. 'Just hear me through to the end. Then make your judgement.' He pulled her to him again.

'As you know,' he started, 'my parents lived abroad for most of my childhood and youth. I had no home, no base in England. When I was a medical student your father took pity on me and invited me to lodge with him and become part of your family. For a while things were wonderful. Everyone made me feel at home—you were particularly nice to me, I remember.'

'I had a crush on you,' interrupted Kate.

'You were sweet. I became very fond of you and looked forward to the times we spent together. You made me feel important. It was rather glamorous having such a pretty young thing watching me with such adoring eyes.'

'So you noticed. Conceited man!'

'Hush, woman. That was the nice bit. Now I'm getting to the horrible bit. Where the wicked stepmother puts an end to everyone's happiness.'

'Julia,' said Kate.

'The very one,' said David, bitterness creeping into his voice for the first time. 'At first she, too, was wonderful and welcoming. A real mother figure—or so I thought. Then I noticed how she frequently engineered occasions when she and I would be alone together in the house.

'She was always wanting me to examine her, convinced she had all sorts of ailments. I protested, saying I was only a medical student and that as she was married to a doctor wasn't it more appropriate she should tell him? But she'd nearly go hysterical whenever I suggested that. Her excuse was she didn't want to worry your father. He would make such a fuss and drive her mad, sending her for all kinds of unnecessary tests.

'At first I took it at face value and thought maybe she just had a bad case of hypochondria. So just to keep her happy I would check her blood pressure, take her pulse, listen to her heart—all that sort of thing.

'At one stage she was convinced she had a heart murmur. Then she thought she had a melanoma on her thigh. High up on her thigh. She had to pull her skirt right up to show me. Of course it was just a tiny scratch, nothing wrong with her at all. I began to realise she was making it all up, but foolishly went along with her persistent demands for examinations just to pacify her.

'Then, on that dreadful day when your father came home early, Julia had called me into her bedroom, saying she was worried she might have breast cancer. Would I please examine her for a lump? By now I was feeling distinctly uncomfortable about the whole thing. I was an inexperienced young man but I knew a vamp when I saw one. Yet on that particular day I could see no way out of the situation. I felt trapped. Julia was almost in tears. She was a very highly strung woman.'

'You can say that again,' Kate interjected, recalling the tantrums she'd often witnessed from her stepmother.

'She had apparently just had a bath,' continued David. 'She was wearing only a nylon waist slip and a flimsy negligee, which she slipped off for the examination. She was naked above the waist. At her insistence I started to feel around her breast for lumps. Then out of the blue she grabbed me and started kissing me, moaning and writhing against me, saying, "Take me! Take me!" I was completely thrown off guard and thoroughly confused—too much manly pride to run away, too physically repelled by her predatory seduction technique to do what she wanted.

'At that moment your father walked in the room. She must have seen him a fraction of a second before I did. She began to struggle, pushing me away, screaming, "Let me go, let me go."'

David shuddered at the recollection. 'The scene

was like something out of a bedroom farce. There framed in the doorway was your stricken father, there on the bed was a half-naked woman ostensibly struggling for her virtue. And there was I, a lusty young medical student groping the professor's wife. Things didn't look good, I can tell you!'

For the first time during the telling of the tale David relaxed. 'It makes me laugh to think how naïve I must have been. Not only did I let her draw me into her web so easily, I actually imagined that my stammering explanation would be believed by your father.

'However, my dear Kate, that is the truth, the whole truth and nothing but the truth. The question is, do you believe me? Or do you still believe your father?'

Kate had listened with mounting disgust at the way Julia had allegedly lured David into her trap. Trying to look at it dispassionately, Kate wondered if David was telling the truth. Was it her father who had got the story wrong?

It took some minutes before Kate spoke. Was David's story believable? Could her stepmother have been to blame all along?

'You do believe me, don't you, Kate?' David was unable to conceal the anxiety in his voice.

She turned to him. He looked so miserable, waiting for her reply, not knowing who she would side with—him or her father.

Of course, he could be lying, rationalised Kate, just to get me where he wants me. Is he just a very good actor, or is he genuine?

'Believe me,' he almost begged. 'Believe me, my love.'

This time Kate let her heart rule her head.

'I believe you.'

As she said the words he had been longing to hear, relief swept over his entire body. He took her face in his hands and, bending his head over her, kissed her once more, as the last rays of the sun slipped behind the mountain range.

Back at the surgery, David carried her small overnight bag, the one he'd packed three days previously.

'Hope you had everything you needed,' he said, referring to it as they walked into the house. 'Packing was never my strong point.'

'You did magnificently,' she replied magnanimously. 'You seemed to know just what a woman needs for an overnight stay, even down to the make-up bag you thoughtfully threw in!'

'I put that in as an afterthought—I wasn't sure whether you'd need it. Someone with skin and hair as beautiful as yours can probably get away with just soap and water,' he said gallantly.

'Don't you believe it.' Kate laughed as they climbed the stairs. 'You should see me first thing in the morning!'

'Now, that's an offer I'm not going to refuse!' he said, throwing her a wicked glance. 'Which reminds me. I'm determined to take you up on that promise to come fell-walking with me. How about this weekend?'

'Sounds great,' replied Kate.

'I'll take you up Scafell Pike. It's a long walk but

we'll take it slowly, camping overnight to fit in two full days' walking. How does that sound?'

To Kate it sounded magical. 'Fine,' she said. 'I'll look forward to it.'

He handed her the bag, and went up to his own flat. 'Welcome back,' he threw at her over his shoulder.

After the practice meeting next morning, David fell into step with Kate on the way to her consulting room. 'About the weekend,' he said. 'I've got all gear—tent, sleeping bags, all the Boy Scout stuff—so you needn't rush out and buy anything.'

'Dr Firth,' said Tracy, cupping her hand over the phone. 'Personal call for you. Shall I put it through to your room?'

He stopped and turned. 'Who is it, Tracy?'

'Someone called Maria.'

'Yes, I'll take it in my own room.' He walked briskly into his consulting room and closed the door.

Kate, who up to that moment had been feeling on top of the world with the prospect of a romantic weekend in the hills with David, now felt the unpleasant stab of an unfamiliar emotion. At the mention of Maria's name, Kate felt something very close to jealousy.

Maria was the glamorous brunette who, as far as Kate was concerned, had spent the entire mountain rescue glued to David's side, the sexy siren who had kept snuggling up to him and gazing into his eyes.

She was also the woman Kate had overheard fixing up a date to see him on Wednesday. That's today, Kate realised with a jolt. So, he's going out on a date with that woman tonight, after arranging to spend the weekend with me. No doubt at this precise moment he's fixing up a time and place for their tryst. 'Maria's a married woman,' he'd said with indignation at Kate's earlier accusation. Married woman she might be, but that didn't stop her setting her cap at David. And, apparently, it didn't stop him responding to her siren call.

Kate gritted her teeth, furious for allowing herself such small-minded, jealous thoughts. Leaning back in her chair, she shook her head, letting her hair float loosely round her shoulders. What can you expect with someone like David? Such an impossibly handsome man is bound to attract a whole bevy of women, like moths round a flame. Was Kate just another moth queueing up to burn herself on the flame of his passion?

She pressed her intercom. 'Tracy, would you please send in my first patient?'

Later that day, in the lull before the evening clinic, Kate phoned her father for a chat. The door of her consulting room was open and she saw David walk past. He saw she was on the phone and gave a perfunctory wave. He was smartly dressed and obviously on his way out somewhere. On his way out somewhere intimate and candlelit, surmised Kate.

'I'm sorry, Dad, what was that you were saying? My mind wandered off for a minute.'

Try as she might, Kate just couldn't rid herself of the jealousy she felt. The green-eyed monster. That was the one emotion to which she'd believed she'd never succumb—it was so destructive, so pointless.

If you can't trust someone, she would tell herself, better not get involved in the first place.

Easier said than done, she now realised. Never before had she felt such passion for a man, such overwhelming need and desire for him. Never before had she felt such possessiveness. She wanted him as much as he wanted her. The only difference being that for Kate he was the only one—whereas, as far as David was concerned, was she to be just one among many?

Thursday and Friday seemed to speed by, so busy were they at the practice. The hayfever season had started early and there was a spate of call-outs for asthmatic emergencies. Then a visit to a local old people's home to check on the residents' health took up most of Friday afternoon for Kate. On her way back into the practice she met David in Reception.

'All set for an early start tomorrow?' he said. 'I'm just on my way out to buy some provisions.'

A practical thought struck Kate. 'Do I need to bring any food with me for the weekend?'

'I'll get everything,' he said, leaping down the surgery steps. 'Just bring yourself, some Kendal Mint Cake and all the energy you can muster. You'll need it!'

'Hope you went to bed early last night,' said David, as they drove out of the practice car park early on Saturday morning. 'Don't want you flagging halfway through the day.'

'Yes, Doctor. I took your advice and was tucked up in bed by ten.'

He raised an eyebrow. 'Doing what I tell you at last. There's hope for me yet.'

Kate settled herself comfortably into the car seat. 'Have you ever been up Helvellyn?' she asked.

'Dozens of times. Why do you ask?'

'Oh, it's just that Gareth was talking about it last week. He said it was a nice walk.'

At the mention of Gareth's name David stiffened. 'I meant to ask you about that,' he said brusquely.

'About Helvellyn?'

'About Gareth. Are you going out with him?'

Kate laughed lightly. 'I've been *out* with him a couple of times, if that's what you're getting at. Three times, if you count the mountain rescue.'

'You know very well what I mean.' David's tone was serious. 'Are you involved with him? Does he consider you to be his girlfriend? You know exactly what I'm talking about, Kate. Don't play with words.'

'No, David, I'm not his *girlfriend*. I'm not anyone's *girlfriend*. You make it sound like I'm a possession, a chattel, to be owned by some bloke.'

'Gareth certainly gave me the impression you were, shall we say, *in his area of interest* when I met you both off the Ullswater ferry. All that business of "take care of her, David" was intended to warn me off.'

'It didn't work, though, did it?' said Kate mischievously.

'I've told you before, nothing stands in my way when I've set my mind on something, or somebody. I just wondered whether this was going to be the end of a beautiful friendship as far as Gareth and I were concerned.'

Kate decided she had better clear the air. After all, the two men did have to work together, preferably in harmony, on the mountain rescue emergencies. She mustn't put that relationship at risk.

'Relax, David. Gareth and I are just good friends. As they say.'

Slamming the car into low gear, David steered it up a steep incline. Was that a look of triumph or relief she detected? Whatever it was, it stung her into action.

'While we're on the subject,' she challenged, 'I think you've a little explaining to do yourself—about Wednesday night.'

'Wednesday night?'

'Don't come over all innocent, David. I know you went out with Maria on Wednesday night. Don't deny it.'

'Of course I don't deny it.'

His ready admission took Kate's breath away. 'You don't? You rat! And you have the nerve to cross-examine me about other men when you're carrying on with another woman.'

'Hey, hang on a minute.' David laughed. 'On Wednesday, yes, I was with Maria. No, we weren't "carrying on" or having an affair, as you seem to suggest.'

'What other reason could you possibly have for going out with her, then?' snarled Kate. 'She's hardly the kind of woman who'd want to play bingo all night, that's for sure.'

'Maria asked me to give a talk on the medical

aspects of mountain rescue to a group of young people who are keen to join as volunteers.'

Kate's silence amused David. He reached for her hand and gave it a playful squeeze. 'Nice to know I can arouse the same fierce feelings of jealousy in you that you definitely arouse in me, particularly when I was convinced you were involved with Gareth. I might even have come to blows with him over you. So much for my Hippocratic oath!'

They started their walk in the small hamlet of Seathwaite, at the head of Borrowdale. 'The wettest inhabited place in the country,' David informed her as they parked the car on a grassy verge near some farm buildings.

Fortunately, the area wasn't living up to its reputation that day and there wasn't a cloud in the sky.

They put on their rucksacks. David's was considerably larger and bulkier than Kate's.

'I feel really guilty, making you carry all that gear,' she said. 'Is it very heavy?'

'Not really,' he replied, hitching the pack more comfortably on his shoulders and fastening the hip strap. 'It's all a matter of balance. The secret of a good rucksack lies in the way the frame and the holster distribute the weight. As with all the gear connected with hillwalking, the more waterproof it is and the lighter it is, the more it costs.' He gave her a wry look. 'Going by that criterion, according to the price I paid for this it should almost carry itself.'

Kate drew in great draughts of the clear mountain air and surveyed the scene around her. Mountains and peaks towered in all directions, intensely green valleys contrasting with bare rugged crags. 'This is so beautiful!' she marvelled.

'There are several routes up Scafell Pike,' said David after they had been walking for a few minutes. 'The one we're taking is, in my opinion, the best, with some of the finest mountain-walking in the Lake District. This particular Borrowdale route lets you see more of the Scafell range of mountains than any other. And though it's not an easy walk, it's certainly easier than some of the other routes up Scafell Pike which are more appropriate for mountain goats than fell-walkers.

'This way is also the prettiest,' he added, 'and it gives us the added advantage of two contrasting routes, one for the way up and a different one on the way down.' He glanced at her sideways. 'I'd better stop lecturing you,' he said, embarrassed by his own enthusiasm. 'I'm turning into a mountain bore.'

'Please, keep telling me about it,' said Kate, exhilarated by his exuberance. 'I know so little about the area and find it fascinating to hear about it. You're not boring me at all.'

Seeing his own enthusiasm reflected in her shining eyes, he stopped walking and placed a kiss between her eyebrows.

They took the broad footpath by the side of the River Derwent, past Stockley Bridge and along a path that started to climb by a small stream. As they got higher, the massive bulk of the Great End mountain appeared over the lip of the land.

They left the quiet beauty of the valley pastures and woods behind them as the rugged wildness of the peaks and mountains beckoned them onwards and upwards.

The towering precipice of Great End increasingly dominated their vista and by the time they had reached Ruddy Gill, with its eponymous red subsoil, the mountain had assumed awe-inspiring proportions. They stopped for a coffee-break, unhitching their rucksacks and leaning against them.

'Never thought instant coffee could taste so good,' said Kate, gulping it down gratefully.

David cupped his hands round the cup of hot, black liquid. 'Caffeine's a wonderful drug. At the right time and place.'

After swigging his coffee, he pointed in the direction of a misty mountain range. 'That's Great Gable, but the best view is over here.'

He turned her round to face the direction from where they had just come. She felt his strong hands firmly on her shoulders, warm and powerful and just as wonderful as the scenery.

Looking down the mountainside in the direction he was pointing her, Kate could see the glorious vista of Derwentwater stretching out below.

After a ten-minute rest they packed their flask and cups away and headed upwards again, following the track towards Esk Hause, in the shadow of the Great End mountain and its scree slopes.

Throughout the day they walked onwards and upwards, along some of the highest Lakeland footpaths. On Esk Hause, a grass plateau high in the mountains, they stopped for lunch—cheese and pickle barm cakes, a Mars bar and an apple each.

'This is so good,' said Kate, tucking into her picnic lunch with relish. 'Why does food taste so much better up a mountain in the open air?'

'Somebody could probably write a thesis on that,' suggested David in between mouthfuls. 'I'm sure some bread company or multinational organisation could be persuaded to put up the sponsorship money for a research fellowship into the subject. It sounds so tempting I could be persuaded to apply for it myself, if it ever came to pass.'

'What, and leave the love of your life—general practice?' said Kate in a similar jocular vein.

'When you said the love of my life just then,' said David, peering at her with penetrating eyes, 'I thought you might have been talking about yourself.'

Although her heart was racing, Kate said nothing, letting the moment pass. Instead she bit into the thick, soft chocolate bar.

She found it increasingly difficult to know when David was serious or joking. There was nothing she desired more than to be the love of his life, but putting it the way he had just now made her unsure. They were having a jokey conversation after all. It was hardly the moment for him to declare undying love.

During the afternoon they continued their climb upwards towards the towering presence of Scafell Pike, past cairns, gullies and ravines, taking in superb clifftop views.

As they walked along David pointed out various interesting features with names that sounded weird and wonderful to Kate. There were so many names Kate could hardly remember any of them. The only one she was sure of was Scafell Pike which, as David had told her, was the highest point of a lofty mountain range which included four summits, all of them exceeding three thousand feet in height. Together they formed the most formidable mountain barrier in the Lake District, most of it a rough, rocky desert of stones.

As the day wore on Kate began to tire. 'I don't think I've got the energy to go to the top of *that.*' She nodded in the direction of Scafell Pike, menacing and glowering, the focal point and pinnacle of their walk.

'We're not going up it today, my love, so don't worry. We'll tackle it tomorrow when we're fresh. That's why I thought it would be a good idea to camp overnight. The last thing any walker wants is to tackle the toughest climb at the end of the day.'

He pointed out a spot on the map to her. 'This is where we're now heading—a place called Hollow Stones. It's an excellent place to bivouac, with lots of big boulders to pitch a small tent behind for shelter. Then, in the morning, we can watch the sun rising over Scafell Crag.'

'How much further to this Hollow Stones place?' asked Kate, hoping to disguise the fact that she was now feeling very tired and ready to pack it in for the day.

'Just a little further on, that's all, near an area called Mickledore.'

They stopped for a tea-break and another apple, regaining enough energy for the final push of the day.

They were rewarded twenty minutes later as they stood on the narrow ridge linking the two peaks of Scafell and Scafell Pike in a place of awesome grandeur amid high and dramatic mountain scenery. Massive towers of naked rock soared majestically into the sky on all sides.

'They say that if you stand here on a clear day, you're granted a free pass into the home of the gods,' said David. 'It certainly makes you feel insignificant, looking out on a scene that hasn't changed for millions of years.'

They took the footpath down from Mickledore and into the snug, sheltered area of Hollow Stones.

Dumping their rucksacks on the ground, they lay down, their backs against a smooth rock, and took a well-earned breather. While Kate was still enjoying the rest, soaking up the last rays of the sun, David set to and pitched the small peapod tent.

'It could be a bit of a squash in here tonight, I should warn you,' said David apologetically. 'Officially this is a one-man tent. But I reckoned if it's made to accommodate the bulky bodies of some of the larger hillwalkers I've seen up here, then it could surely fit in one medium-sized man and one very slim girl. At a pinch.'

'No pinching allowed,' said Kate, languidly stretching her aching limbs.

David pulled out two down-filled sleeping bags which had been packed into a minuscule space in his rucksack.

'Dr Marshall, you have a decision to make,' he said, shaking them out. From being tiny, crumpled objects, they fluffed up to normal-sized sleeping bags. 'You can have your own individual sleeping bag. Or we can unzip them, turning them into a top quilt and bottom quilt and making a very comfortable double bed. It's like sleeping between two luxury duvets. But you can choose which you'd rather have.'

'Perhaps you'd better talk me through the advantages and disadvantages of each,' replied Kate teasingly.

'As far as I am aware, there are absolutely no advantages in keeping them as single bags, whereas if unzipped, thus...' he demonstrated '...placing one over the other, the sleeping bags take up much less room in this very small tent.'

'I see,' said Kate, outwardly amused and inwardly excited at the prospect of the night ahead. 'So space-saving considerations are, as far as you are concerned, the only reason for putting together the aforementioned sleeping bags?'

'Good heavens, woman,' said David, keeping a serious face. 'I do hope you aren't thinking I have any ulterior motive in suggesting such a course of action?'

Less than half an hour later they were eating their evening meal—tinned beans and sausages, heated over a tiny gas stove, accompanied by a bottle of exquisite red wine which David had miraculously produced from his rucksack, along with two glasses.

Kate swore it was the best meal she had ever eaten.

Presently, it was time to go to bed. Once the sun had disappeared behind the mountains, the night air became chilly. By contrast, inside the small tent it was snug and warm.

They stripped off their clothes with an urgency

born of desire, and slipped under the cosy warmth of the goose-down quilts. Kate got in first. It was like lying on a soft feather bed. She snuggled sensually into the quilts' luxurious embrace.

David slid down behind her, placing one hand over her midriff, the other round her breasts.

He pressed a soft kiss on her neck and gently moved his lips to the lobe of her ear. 'This is the best part of the walk for me. I've thought of little else all the way up the mountain.'

'Yes,' she sighed, catching her breath as, in the intimate darkness of the tent, his hands began to explore her body.

His skin was hot, his body hard and firm, as he pulled her to him. 'Kate, do you want me as much as I want you?' he asked, a husky desperation in his voice.

'Oh, yes, I want you, David,' she whispered as she moved round to face him.

They kissed hungrily, passionately, like two wild creatures, ferocious in their need for each other.

They made love with an intensity she could not have believed possible, each taking the other to unimaginable heights of pleasure. David groaned, his breathing tortured, as her nails dug into his back.

Kate shed all inhibitions, oblivious to where they were. All that mattered was that moment, that sublime moment when she reached the pinnacle of her pleasure, plunging her face into his warm, bare shoulder, tasting the salt of his body on her lips, calling out his name as the frenzy mounted.

When Kate opened her eyes the next day she had absolutely no idea what time it might be. She could tell it was morning from the daylight streaking through the thin green nylon of the tent.

She moved lethargically, feeling David's body curled round behind hers, deep in slumber.

Hardly surprising he's still asleep, she thought, smiling secretly to herself. Neither of them had allowed the other much sleep the previous night. They had made love into the early hours until, finally exhausted, they had fallen asleep curled up in each other's arms.

She lay still, savouring the unaccustomed cosiness of sleeping in the arms of a man, recalling every detail of their love-making, every passionate word he had whispered. How she wished he'd said he loved her. And then she could have told him she loved him.

Feeling him stir, she quickly pushed these thoughts to the back of her mind. Desire rose in her veins at the touch of his body against hers. She moved sensually against him, taking delight in the arousing effect she knew her body was having on his.

Waking up as the flames of desire licked through him, he moved his hands over her, caressing her with new urgency, turning her to face him.

His body moved over hers and once more she felt the delicious weight of him on her as last night's passion flared into new life.

CHAPTER NINE

'I DIDN'T expect breakfast in bed, that's for sure,' said Kate, biting into the rather squashed but very delicious croissant David had handed to her along with a cup of steaming black coffee.

'You'd be surprised what I've got in that rucksack,' he said enigmatically.

Shortly after their love-making that morning, David had slipped out of the tent, leaving Kate a few more moments of bliss, luxuriating in the warmth and softness of the down-filled quilts.

Some time later he appeared at the tent opening with her breakfast. He told her he had sprinted, naked apart from his boots and towel, to a nearby tarn where he'd splashed himself with icy water, before shaving and getting dressed.

He looked as fresh and groomed as he had at the start of their walk.

'If you think I'm sprinting naked to bathe in some freezing pool, you've another think coming.' Kate shuddered at the very idea, popping the last of the croissant into her mouth.

'Pity,' said David. 'I was rather looking forward to it. I'd got my camera out specially.'

Kate eased herself out of the seductive warmth of the sleeping bags and pulled on her clothes, her only concession to civilisation being fresh underwear. 'I'll splash water on my face and clean my teeth at this tarn of yours. That will have to do until I get back home and can soak in a nice bath!'

As she joined David outside the tent, the landscape that greeted her took her breath away. The sun was just rising behind the vast face of Scafell Crag, bathing it in a rosy hue, transforming its harsh, black silhouette into a soft, pink castle.

They sat together, watching the scene unfold before their eyes, a scene that had not changed since the dawn of time.

'I've only ever seen it like this once before,' he said. 'More often than not it rains whenever I decide to come up here.'

They packed their gear and set off in the direction of Broad Crag and the path leading to Scafell Pike. The walking wasn't easy—the path being covered in scree and rough blocks of stone. Kate needed all her wits about her to avoid twisting an ankle or slipping downhill.

'This is the final climb,' said David encouragingly, giving her a helping hand up the last arduous section of the path.

They stood at the top of the mountain, the only people there. Kate experienced an enormous sense of achievement. She felt on top of the world.

It was a beautiful, clear morning and they had magnificent views in all directions, from the Isle of Man to the Yorkshire Pennines. Stretching out to the south was a magnificent lake.

'Wast Water,' said David. 'The deepest lake and one of the most unspoiled. And, as I mentioned before, the scene of my conception.'

They removed their rucksacks, propping them

against a large cairn near the Ordnance Survey trig point, the column which marked the highest point on the mountain, a remnant of the days when mapmakers travelled on foot, not in aeroplanes.

Holding her hands in his, David looked deep into her eyes. 'Kate, this is a very special place to me. I had to bring you here, even though it's hardly a suitable choice for your first real mountain walk. But I couldn't wait any longer for us to be together on this spot.

'I brought you here to ask you to marry me. I love you so much. I have since the moment I set eyes on you again in the surgery waiting room. It was like seeing the woman of my dreams walking into my life. When I discovered who you were I tried desperately to keep away from you. But it was hopeless. In the end I realised that there was no way I was going to be able to stay away.'

Kate's heart lurched. For a moment she couldn't answer, so unexpected had his proposal been.

'Please, marry me, Kate,' persisted David. 'If I can't have you, my life is worthless. I thought I'd die if I couldn't persuade you of the truth about my past.'

'Yes, David,' she said happily. 'Of course I'll marry you. You're the only man I've ever loved. I think I did all along, even when I thought you had tried to seduce Julia. I just hated myself for loving you.'

He made a hoarse sound in his throat, a combination of relief, desire and happiness all rolled into one. His arms enveloped her, holding her close, pressing her body to his, as his mouth came down on hers.

They kissed deeply and wildly, oblivious to all else. Kate's pulses hammered at her throat and chest. Her hand clasped the back of his head, arching her body against him as he angled his strong muscular thigh between her legs.

'I want you so desperately,' he said raggedly. 'I can hardly believe you're going to be mine.' He leaned back and, lifting his face to the heavens, bellowed to the sky, 'Kate Marshall is going to marry me!'

Kate laughed with joy. It was the happiest day of her life, standing there on the very rooftop of England, in the arms of the man she loved.

David bent down to his rucksack and pulled out a small box.

'I said you'd be surprised at what I've brought in this rucksack,' he said, opening the box to reveal an exquisite solitaire diamond ring.

'I know engagements are old-fashioned,' he said, slipping it on her finger. It was an almost perfect fit. 'But, then, I am rather old-fashioned. I believe in all those old-fashioned things like true love and destiny and motherhood and apple pie...'

'David, it's beautiful,' gasped Kate, thrilled at the ring that now glittered and sparkled on the third finger of her left hand. 'Do you mean to say you bought this, and hiked it all the way up here, on the off chance I'd say yes?'

'Absolutely,' said David. 'It's been a secret ambition of mine to propose on top of Scafell Pike.' He hugged her to him, kissing the top of her head. 'Precious girl. I bought the ring in a mad moment on Friday. If you'd turned me down, I'd just have thrown myself off the top of the mountain.'

They stood in silence, savouring their special moment. Then Kate began to think ahead.

'David, would you mind if we keep it a secret for just a little while? I'm dreading telling my father. I need time to work on him and persuade him you're not the ogre he thinks you are.'

'Of course, darling,' he said with understanding. 'I'm so happy right now I'd agree to anything you asked. Only don't make me keep it a secret for too long. I'm crazy about you and I want us to be married as soon as possible. If that means getting married without your father's blessing then that's what we'll have to do.'

He saw a look of dismay cloud her face.

'That is what we'll do, isn't it, Kate? You agreeing to marry me isn't conditional on your father giving me the thumbs-up? You'll have to make a choice. Him or me.'

'There's no choice to be made, David. I love you. I'd run away and live with you in a crofter's hut in the Outer Hebrides if necessary, but right now I must go gently with my father so soon after his brain operation. Let me tell him in my own time, in my own way.'

He kissed her again, with gentle caressing lips, his hands clasping her face. 'Of course, my love. But just remember, I'm not a patient man.'

The way down the mountain was, of course, much quicker and easier than the climb up. David and Kate took it at their leisure, enjoying the scenery and each other's company.

'What about your family?' she asked. 'Are your parents still alive?'

'Yes, both of them, I'm happy to say. Father is now retired and they live in Dorset. It's the first real home they've had in England after all those years of living abroad.'

'Do you have any other brothers or sisters, apart from Roger?' she enquired, now very keen to know all about his family, the family she would soon be marrying into.

'Just Roger,' he replied. 'My mother had several miscarriages and considered herself lucky to end up with two children. She always wanted a daughter, and was thrilled when Roger and his wife Helen produced their first baby six months ago—a little girl called Fiona. She's a little sweetie. Which reminds me,' he said turning to her. 'Talking of babies, I saw Jenny last week.'

'How is she?' said Kate, who had often thought about David's partner and the baby she had delivered on her first day as locum.

'In fine fettle. And the baby is thriving. She's called Kate, after you. Jenny said she'd like you to call in and see her some time. I'll let you have her address and phone number when we get back to the practice.'

The door of the pretty Lakeland stone cottage was opened even before Kate could reach for the bell.

'I've just got her off to sleep,' said Jenny in a

conspiratorial whisper. 'Creep in quietly so as not to wake her.'

The baby was asleep in her pram in the hallway, and Kate managed to steal a peep as she walked past. 'She looks angelic,' she said in a low voice to Jenny as she followed her into the large, welcoming kitchen.

'Looks can be deceptive as far as babies are concerned,' said Jenny ruefully, filling the kettle. 'Tea or coffee?'

'Coffee would be lovely,' replied Kate, seating herself at the scrubbed pine table in the centre of the cosy room.

'I'm sticking to herb tea while I'm still breast-feeding,' said Jenny. 'So, tell me all the news from the practice. Coping all right in your first posting as a GP?'

'I love it, Jenny,' enthused Kate. 'I'm so glad I made the decision to go into general practice. It's just what I was cut out for. There's such a variety of work and patients, so much more interesting than being stuck in a big hospital.'

'And how are you getting on with Gordon and David? I hope they're being perfect gentlemen as well as perfect doctors. They can be a bit pig-headed when they think their way of doing things is the best—particularly David. I thought it was priceless when he mistook you for a patient and bit your head off, just after you'd done a magnificent job of delivering my daughter!'

'I get on remarkably well with both of them,' said Kate, longing to confide in Jenny just *how* well she was getting on with David. However, for the time being she had to keep her mouth shut on that particular subject, certainly until she'd broken the news to her father.

'I'm glad you said that.' Jenny handed Kate a mug of coffee. 'In that case I have something I want to talk over with you. First I had to discover how the land lies, so to speak.'

'You're being very mysterious,' said Kate, sipping the hot liquid.

'How do you feel about staying on permanently at the practice when your six-month contract is up?'

Kate was taken aback. 'You mean, join the partnership? I wouldn't have thought there was a big enough patient list to justify four full-time doctors.'

'There isn't. I'm asking you if you're interested in taking my place.'

'But I thought you were looking forward to coming back when the baby was six months old. That was what you had in mind, wasn't it?'

'It was what I had in mind before I had the baby. Once she was born I began to feel quite differently about it.'

Their conversation was interrupted by a noise from the hall. Baby Kate had woken up and was making her presence felt.

'She can be a little monster, even though I adore her,' said Jenny, going out to pacify her daughter. As soon as Jenny picked her up she stopped crying quite so loudly and whimpered instead, her tiny face wrinkled up in a deep frown.

'Madam is not pleased,' said Jenny, putting the cross infant over her shoulder and patting her gently on the back. 'Feeding on demand is all very well, but what do you do with someone as demanding as this?'

Jenny settled herself down in a comfortable armless chair in the corner of the kitchen and began to unbutton her shirt. Once the little mouth was attached to her nipple and the baby was suckling greedily, Jenny continued her conversation with Kate.

'Before you have a baby you have no idea how much it will alter your life. How much they take over your entire existence. And how they awaken feelings in you that you never imagined you had. Deep, primitive, maternal feelings that force themselves to the surface and almost overwhelm you with their intensity.'

Jenny looked down lovingly at the round, silken-haired head as the small mouth sucked rhythmically at her breast.

'I just can't bear the thought of leaving her for someone else to look after. Not while she's so small. Not even at six months. I will still want to breast-feed her. She needs me and I need her—for these first precious months, at least.

'By the time she's a toddler I'm sure I'll be very glad to get back to some kind of work. What I think I'd like to do then is to come back part time—perhaps do the odd clinic one or two afternoons a week. But the practice will need a third full-time doctor.'

'Have you mentioned this to Gordon or David yet?' Kate asked.

'No, I thought I'd better check it out with you first, then I can give them the two pieces of news at once. That I'm not coming back—and that you are staying!'

'They may not want me on a permanent basis,' said Kate. 'Have you thought about that?'

'Oh, yes, they would!' said Jenny with conviction. 'I know it for a fact. Gordon raves about you—and David thinks you're the best doctor since medical degrees were handed out. So what's your answer, Dr Marshall? Are you prepared to forgo the allure of the bright city lights and join a bunch of country doctors?'

'There's nothing I'd like more,' replied Kate, her eyes flicking over to where the baby was snuggled in Jenny's arms.

Nothing I'd like more, except a baby of my own.

If she was honest, given the choice between general practice and holding David's baby in her arms, Kate knew without a doubt that general practice would have to take second place.

Kate walked through the now familiar doors of the Birmingham hospital. It was hard to believe it was only two weeks ago she had first entered the place. Then she had been numb with fear and anxiety for her father in his desperate plight before his brain operation. Now she was walking with a much lighter heart, looking forward to bringing him home to Cheshire to continue his recuperation.

Before setting off from the Lakes, Kate had been struck by a worrying thought. Although she had done her best to conceal from her father the fact that she had met up again with David, she had completely forgotten to mention the awkwardness of the situation to Roger Firth.

It was entirely feasible that once Dr Marshall had

recovered sufficiently from the operation he would insist on discussing the whole medical experience with the surgeon. It was also entirely feasible that Roger would tell him how he came to be in his hospital in the first place, through a referral from his brother. When Kate's father discovered his brother's name was David, he would be bound to connect the two names. If that happened, how could Kate explain away her apparent deception?

Rushing into David's room before setting off down the motorway to Birmingham, she had blurted out her concerns.

'Don't worry, my love,' David had said, kissing her goodbye. 'I'd already considered that possibility. I've put Roger in the picture. He won't say a word.'

Kate had breathed a sigh of relief.

'Come back soon, my darling,' he'd said softly in her ear. 'Then we can tell the world we're in love. I hate having to pretend we're just good friends.'

As she greeted her father, Kate felt happy and relaxed, confident in the knowledge that her father hadn't the slightest inkling that the brilliant surgeon who had operated on him was, in fact, the brother of the man he believed had assaulted Julia, his wife.

'All packed and ready to go?' she asked, seeing him perched impatiently on the edge of his chair, a large bandage round his head.

'Can't wait to be home,' he said, rising rather unsteadily to his feet.

The first week at home, caring for her father, passed very quickly. Kate had been fully occupied, taking on the roles of doctor, nurse and housekeeper, not to mention gardener.

In the three weeks since Dr Marshall's collapse, his normally well-kept lawns had deteriorated into an untidy, overgrown mess. Kate could see her father was itching to get out the lawnmower and do the job himself, having turned down Kate's invitation to find him a gardener to take on the work.

'Certainly not!' he'd replied sullenly with all the ill-temper of a small boy stamping his foot in juvenile petulance.

'My garden is my delight,' he'd said. 'I'm not having someone stomping around it, pulling up things they shouldn't, stepping on precious seedlings.'

So Kate ended up mowing the lawn herself under the eagle eye of her father, who insisted on giving detailed instructions on how high the cutter blades should be, how close it should be mown to the edge, how straight the lines must be... She had never realised there was so much to it. Up till then Kate had thought mowing a lawn was, well, just mowing a lawn.

As for dealing with the flower-beds, she was allowed to do a bit of dead heading and weeding—but, again, only under her father's penetrating gaze. After ten days of this scrutiny Kate was looking forward to returning to the comparative tranquillity of the practice, which had its own share of truculent patients.

She loved her father dearly, and realised he was only acting that way out of sheer frustration. For a man as active as he had previously been, this enforced rest was driving him mad. He had been told not to read any medical textbooks or to do anything remotely connected with work for at least another month. He wasn't to return to his teaching job until the start of the new academic year.

The thought of nearly six months' enforced 'house arrest', as he called it, was turning him into a bad-tempered, impatient old grumbler. Kate hadn't the heart to tackle him about it, but she knew that if she had to stay with him for much longer things would soon come to a head.

Awkward old cuss that he was at the moment, Kate had, however, managed to persuade him to use the services of a district nurse who would visit him on a daily basis, keeping an eye on him and attending to his dressing once Kate was no longer around.

'I don't want some interfering old busybody poking her nose in here, telling me what to do,' grumbled Dr Marshall.

'I'd like to see someone telling *you* what to do,' said Kate ruefully, wrapping the new dressing round his head. 'Anyway, that's what you've agreed. Nurse Hoyle will come and visit you once a day just to do this dressing, because you know very well you can't do it yourself. And I have to get back to my job or they may not keep it open for me. Nurse Hoyle's coming along today to introduce herself so be nice to her. Don't let me down. Promise?'

'Yes, my dear,' said Dr Marshall. 'I'm very grateful the way you rushed down here to look after me. I'll try not to be such a silly old fool. You get back to your job and don't be worrying about me. You know, you still haven't told me an awful lot about the Lake District practice. Tell me about your colleagues. Good doctors, are they?'

As Kate fixed the dressing in place she knew in her heart that now was an ideal opportunity to tell him about David. It was a perfect time to go through the whole story. But somehow she lost her nerve. She just couldn't tell him, not at that precise moment anyway. But, if not now, when? When would she tell him that she was going to marry the very man whom he believed had tried to rape her stepmother?

Each night, after her father had gone to bed, Kate phoned David. It was agony, being apart, and she could tell from the longing in his voice that he was missing her as much as she was missing him.

'I just hope no one's taping this conversation,' said David after one of their late night calls when they'd spoken in uninhibited lovers' language. 'I don't know about you, but after you've called I have to jump under a cold shower the moment I put the receiver down. Anyway, my love, tell your father about us soon. The sooner it's all out in the open, the better.'

Kate finished doing up her father's bandage and recalled guiltily the last words of David's telephone conversation the previous night. 'Have you told him yet?' he'd asked.

'No, but I will tomorrow,' she'd assured him.

'Make sure you do. I'm collecting the ring from the jewellers tomorrow and I shall insist on you wearing it the moment you come back here.'

Kate had pushed the thought of wearing the engagement ring to the back of her mind. The decision had been taken out of her hands initially because the ring had required a small adjustment to make it a secure fit. But she knew that once David got it back he would expect her to wear it. Then the cat would definitely be out of the bag.

While she was agonising over the right moment to tell her father—or, more correctly, when she could summon up enough courage to do so—the doorbell rang. Looking through the kitchen window, Kate saw a small blue car parked on the road, and outside the front door stood the imposing figure of a uniformed district nurse.

'Looks as though Nurse Hoyle has arrived,' announced Kate to Dr Marshall's retreating form as he hastily disappeared into his beloved garden.

Kate brought Nurse Hoyle through to the back garden to meet her father, who seemed determined to cut as independent a figure as possible. He was bending over a clump of flowers, deep in contemplation.

'Ah, Nurse Hoyle,' he said, standing upright and holding out his hand in greeting. 'Dr Marshall. Delighted to meet you, dear lady.'

Kate held back a smile. Her father was now being charm itself. She knew it was all an act, but she was grateful that he wasn't going to let her down by behaving badly.

'"Mrs Kendal Clark", I presume?' said Nurse Hoyle, looking at both Kate and Dr Marshall.

'No,' said Kate. 'I'm Kate Marshall. This is my father. I thought I told you all this on the phone.'

Kate was somewhat taken aback to discover that her father and Nurse Hoyle now dissolved into peals of laughter. It was like a conspiracy. The two of them appeared to be sharing some kind of joke that left

Kate out in the cold. She was completely baffled. Had they both gone mad?

'No, Kate,' said Dr Marshall between guffaws, trying to regain his composure. 'This good lady was referring to this particularly lovely clump of hardy geraniums. Isn't that so, Nurse Hoyle?'

'Indeed.' Nurse Hoyle turned her attention to a bushy plant that grew about eighteen inches high and was covered in a mass of attractive slate-blue flowers. 'Geranium "Mrs Kendal Clark" is my favourite plant in the whole world,' she enthused.

A beam of genuine delight crossed Dr Marshall's face. 'Do you know,' he said, 'it's *my* all-time favourite plant as well. Isn't that amazing?'

'I'm a bit of a hardy geranium nut, I'm afraid!' said Nurse Hoyle exuberantly. 'I'm a member of all sorts of hardy geranium groups and I grow masses of them from seed. That way you can get all sorts of unusual varieties. You must come round and see my collection, Dr Marshall. I've just got my hands on Geranium pratense striatum,' she said conspiratorially.

'You mean the bicolour variety?' said her father with genuine keenness.

'The very one! Tried to grow it from seed for years but it never bred true. But a friend picked one up for me at a plant hunters' fair and I'm thrilled skinny with it!'

Dr Marshall and Nurse Hoyle were by now oblivious to Kate's presence, so wrapped up were they in horticultural conversation. Kate was amused to see how her father had suddenly changed from putting on a charming act for the benefit of Nurse Hoyle to being genuine charmed by the woman and totally captivated by their common interest in gardening.

'And as I said earlier,' continued Nurse Hoyle, 'I just adore the blue of "Mrs Kendal Clark". It's an almost indescribable colour.'

'I've always loved it because it reminds me of the blue of Kate's eyes, particularly when she was a baby.'

Kate was startled to hear her father speaking so sentimentally. As far as she could remember, he had never mentioned this particular blue flower in the past. But before she could say anything Nurse Hoyle was peering into her eyes and then into her father's.

'Hmmm,' she said, assessing the situation critically. 'I would say, Dr Marshall, that the colour of "Mrs Kendal Clark" is much closer to the colour of your own eyes.'

At this point Kate had to excuse herself and run into the house. The look of childish delight on her father's face as Nurse Hoyle unashamedly buttered him up was something to behold. It made Kate want to burst out laughing. She managed to hold in the giggling fit until she was safely inside the kitchen and out of their hearing. Then she exploded with hysterical laughter.

Dr Marshall saw Nurse Hoyle to her car and arranged a suitable time for her visits each day, starting in three days' time when Kate had left to return to her job.

'She seems a very sensible woman,' said Dr Marshall, joining Kate in the kitchen as the small blue car drove away. 'I'm sure Nurse Hoyle and I will get on fine. She's going to bring me a plant of a very rare double geranium. Oh, yes, she's a very sensible woman, very sensible indeed,' he repeated, a serious look on his face. 'So, what are you grinning at, Kate? Did I say something funny?'

Kate hugged her father and smiled up at him lovingly.

'Oh, Dad! You and your blue eyes!'

That evening her phone call to David did not go well. The first thing he asked her was, 'Have you told him yet?'

She had to confess she hadn't. 'I just don't seem to be able to pluck up the courage, David,' she said, trying to make excuses for her lapse. 'He's recovering so well from his op I'm frightened of doing anything that might put that at risk.'

At the other end of the phone David was fuming. 'If you won't tell him, Kate, I will. I'm coming down this weekend—and if you haven't told him by then, I'm going to tell him myself.'

'For heaven's sake, David,' gasped Kate. 'You can't do that! The shock could give him a stroke or a heart attack!'

'Don't dramatise everything. Just tell him!' said David, putting the phone down.

CHAPTER TEN

'DAD, do you remember me asking about David Firth a few weeks ago?'

At the last moment Kate had summoned up all her courage and decided it was now or never. At any minute she would be leaving the house, her fortnight's leave of absence from the practice over.

'I certainly do,' replied her father. They were both sitting at the kitchen table, having a morning coffee before Kate left. 'I also remember what I told you about him. It's a subject I would rather not discuss if you don't mind.'

He wasn't making it easy, but she ploughed on. 'Have you ever thought you might have been wrong about him? That perhaps it was Julia who was to blame?'

Dr Marshall's hands gripped his coffee-cup, his knuckles turning white. 'Kate, the man was a lecher, a womaniser, a seducer. I saw him with my own eyes.'

'It could have been all Julia's fault,' persisted Kate. 'Maybe she had been pestering him, and not the other way round. Have you ever considered that?'

'I don't want to discuss it any more,' said Dr Marshall stubbornly. 'It all happened a very long time ago. I'd much rather forget the whole episode.'

Having got this far, Kate wasn't going to let the matter rest.

'But have you thought about David Firth?' she probed. 'Have you ever wondered what might have happened to him? To his medical career?'

Dr Marshall was pensive for a few moments. Then, just as he was about to speak, there was a knock on the door. It was Nurse Hoyle.

'Just thought I'd pop in for a moment,' she said, striding in with plastic carrier bags full of plants clutched in her hands. 'I know I don't start officially till tomorrow, but as I was passing I brought these.'

At the sound of her voice Dr Marshall had jumped up and rushed out to the hall to greet her. 'How very kind of you, Nurse Hoyle.'

'Do call me Maggie,' she said, handing him the bags. 'I've popped one or two interesting plant specimens in there. This is the very rare double geranium we talked about...' Her voice trailed off as she followed Dr Marshall into the kitchen. Kate could hear the two of them deep in conversation about plants with long Latin-sounding names, all of it completely lost on her.

Seeing the two coffee-cups on the table, Maggie Hoyle said, 'I do hope I'm not interrupting anything. I won't stay long.'

'Oh, please, do,' encouraged Dr Marshall. 'My daughter was just about to leave anyway, weren't you, Kate? I think I might make myself another cup of coffee. Would you care to join me, Nurse Hoyle...Maggie? And by the way, please, call me Ewan.'

Kate knew when she was beaten. Her moment had passed—for the time being. If she was ever going to discuss David with her father and break the news about their engagement, now certainly wasn't the time to do it.

She said her goodbyes and slipped out of the house, leaving the older couple chatting away happily, hardly noticing her departure.

Her father was under the impression Kate was driving straight back to the Lakes, whereas, in fact, she was heading for the centre of Manchester where she had arranged to meet David from the train.

A couple of nights ago David had announced that he was coming down the next weekend for the christening of Fiona, Roger's and Helen's baby. On the spur of the moment they had decided to have the ceremony the following Sunday. David's parents were going to be staying with Roger and Helen for a few days anyway, and everyone thought it would be an ideal opportunity for a family get-together and to have the christening at the same time.

David had, much to his delight, been asked to be the godfather.

He had decided it was also an ideal opportunity to take Kate with him to meet her future in-laws. It had been arranged that Kate would pick him up from the train on the Saturday after leaving Cheshire so they could drive down together. They had booked a room in a small country hotel near Roger and Helen's house in the leafy suburbs south of Birmingham, a few miles from Stratford-upon-Avon.

Kate waited for David outside the ticket barrier, her emotions in complete confusion. On the one hand she couldn't wait to see him again, to kiss him and hold him. On the other hand she was dreading him asking her, yet again, whether or not she had told her father the news of their engagement.

When he first caught sight of her in the crowd at the station his face broke into a wide smile and he ran towards her. Putting his bag down, he lifted her up and hugged her, her feet leaving the ground as he swung her round like a doll.

'God, I've missed you,' he said, kissing her passionately right there in the middle of the busy station concourse.

It was only as they were in the car and about to drive away from the station car park that he asked her the question she knew she'd have to answer sooner or later.

'What did he say when you told him?' he asked, buckling his seat belt.

When she didn't answer he asked again. 'What did he say? Kate, you did tell him?'

'Not yet,' she whispered in a small strangled voice.

'What? Oh, I don't believe it! I just don't believe it, Kate!'

'I tried to tell him, I really did, but...' To her horror she found great tears welling up in her eyes and plopping onto her lap as she bent her head away from his burning gaze.

Although she hadn't intended to play the part of the weeping woman, her tears had an immediate effect on David. Unclipping his seat belt, he leaned over towards her.

'Kate, my darling, I'm so sorry.' Gently he brushed her hair aside and wiped her tears with the flat of his hand. Then he kissed her softly on the forehead. 'I'm such an unfeeling oaf. You've had enough on your plate, without me making things worse. We'll just forget about it for now.'

'I will tell him, David, honestly I will,' she said, her tears now soaking into the thin cotton of his shirt. 'But not just yet. Perhaps after the christening.'

'That's a good idea,' said David, sitting back in the driver's seat and starting the engine. 'We'll call in on our way back to the Lakes. And I'll be with you this time to make sure you don't bottle out!'

'I thought all babies cried at their christenings,' said David's father, a small, dapper man with greying hair. He peered admiringly at his first grandchild.

'Not this one,' said David, holding her proudly in the crook of his arm. 'Not my little goddaughter.'

'She was so good in church. Not like Roger or you,' said David's mother, who was taller than her husband and strikingly good-looking. 'Honestly Kate, I don't know which of the two of them made the most noise. But we were abroad at the time,' she said with disarming distraction, quite oblivious to the *non-sequitur*. 'Roger's christening was in Malta and David's in Singapore.'

'That's probably why I was screaming,' said David. 'I was saying take me back to England, that's where I belong!'

Kate felt completely at home with David's family. It was as if she'd always known them, they were so warm and welcoming. Helen, Roger's wife, had lost her father the previous year, but her mother was at the christening and Kate found her to be excellent company also. Helen's sister Fiona, after whom the baby had been named, was a lawyer working in London and was the godmother.

It was a beautiful summer's day and they were all out in the garden after the ceremony at the local parish church. Roger was pouring champagne, Helen and Fiona handing round tasty morsels. Everyone was relaxed and happy—David particularly so, refusing to hand over his new charge, at least for the time being.

'Not likely,' he said when anyone tried to take the baby from his arms. 'I've just made some very big promises on behalf of this little girl. I've got to keep her on the straight and narrow and watch over her morals, and all that sort of thing. It's a big responsibility, I can tell you.'

'Your main responsibility, as far as I see it,' said Roger laconically, 'is to buy her exceedingly expensive birthday presents and to make a simply marvellous speech at her wedding.'

At the mention of the word 'wedding' David looked across at Kate. She blushed. So far David had told no one of their plans, but she knew he wanted to make the announcement to his family while they were all together.

Some minutes later, as Kate was deep in conversation with Helen's mother, she found David at her elbow. 'I've got to speak to you. Now,' he whispered seductively in her ear. 'If you don't break off your conversation immediately, I'm going to ravish you in front of everyone, right here on the lawn.'

Under her linen jacket Kate felt David's hand slip round her waist and move slowly upwards towards her breasts.

'Would you just excuse me a minute?' she said to Helen's mother, and turned to David.

'What is it, you fool?' she said, smiling up at him in the sunshine. His tanned face was closely shaven, his thick, black hair ruffled by the breeze. 'You handsome fool,' she added, a softness creeping into her voice.

'I have the ring in my pocket and want to tell everyone now. Is that OK with you?' He took the diamond ring out of his top pocket, saying, 'Wear it, please.'

David slipped it on the third finger of her left hand, just as he had on top of Scafell Pike. But this time it fitted her finger exactly. It felt perfect, and looked beautiful, the cut of the diamond catching the sunlight and glinting like a twinkling star.

At that moment Kate felt a serene happiness descend on her. 'Yes, please, tell them. Just as long as baby Fiona doesn't think we're upstaging her on her big day. It is her christening after all.'

'She won't mind,' assured David, 'not *my* godchild.' He took Kate by the hand and walked a few paces to the centre of the lawn.

'Ladies and gentlemen, and members of the Firth family.' A great guffaw went up, forcing him to wait till the uproar died down. 'I have an announcement to make,' he said, when at last he could make himself heard.

Conversation petered out as the christening guests turning to look at them both with curiosity.

'Kate and I are getting married.' David beamed at the faces turned towards them.

The chorus of oohs and aahs overwhelmed them

as all the relatives one by one kissed and hugged Kate and David, congratulating them both and admiring Kate's ring.

A champagne toast was drunk to their future happiness. David couldn't stop grinning. 'I'm so pleased that finally our secret is out in the open,' he said to Kate. 'No going back now.'

Kate was thrilled, too, even though at the back of her mind lurked a niggling anxiety. Only when she'd confronted her father, only then could she finally feel total joy about their engagement.

Roger topped up Kate's champagne glass once more and asked how her father was recovering from his operation.

'Brilliantly,' she said, 'thanks to you.'

'All in a day's work,' he said diffidently. 'When you've seen one pilocytic astrocytoma, you've seen them all.'

'We both know that's not true.' Kate laughed, at last able to take a light-hearted view of her father's illness now that he was well on the road to recovery. 'He's doing so well. In fact, yesterday he was quite happy to dispense with my services. I got the distinct feeling he couldn't wait to get me out of the house.'

'That's the problem with having too many doctors in the family,' said Roger, 'all believing their way of doing things is the best.' He turned to Helen, who had now joined them. 'I have the same trouble myself. Helen's a doctor, a former hospital registrar. It's hell living with a medical know-all.'

'You don't have to tell me, clever clogs,' joked Helen. 'And Kate and David are heading for exactly the same scenario, a two-doctor household. I will say this for it, though, it makes for some very interesting discussions over the dinner table!'

'It can be slightly offputting for one's dinner guests when the host and hostess get into that kind of small talk.' Roger turned to his wife for confirmation. 'Tell them how I upset your mother the other night.'

'It was a bit tactless, you must admit, when you said what a nice shade of mauve her dress was, likening it to the colour of a particular brain you had been operating on that day!'

'Thank you, Roger and Helen,' David butted in. 'You don't need to go into that kind of detail at the moment, even though the garden is knee-deep in medics.'

'As I was saying,' continued Kate, 'my father is doing fine and seems to have found a new interest in life, in the form of a very personable district nurse called Maggie Hoyle. They have discovered a mutual love. It seems they're both mad about "Mrs Kendal Clark".'

'Good heavens,' said Helen, 'who on earth is she?'

'A hardy geranium, apparently.'

'Are you safe to drive?' asked Kate as they walked to the car, having said their goodbyes. 'If you've had as much champers as I have, we'd better call a taxi.'

'What, all the way to the Lakes? Don't worry, I only had a couple of glasses and then went on to orange juice,' said David reassuringly.

'I should have noticed that my glass always seemed to be full,' said Kate, feeling guilty. 'I never saw anyone filling it up. Perhaps you should have had a stern word with me and told me to go easy. I normally do. It's just that, well, today was rather special. And I feel so happy and—' Before she could finish her sentence David had pulled her to him and kissed her.

'I'd no intention of having a stern word with you. You looked so beautiful and happy and I was so proud of you, showing you off to my family.'

They got in the car, but before driving off David checked his watch and said, 'The stern word comes in roughly two hours' time. That's when we'll arrive outside your father's house and when you're going inside to break the news.'

Driving up the motorway, Kate experienced a sinking feeling in her stomach as the euphoria from the champagne gradually wore off.

They arrived outside her father's house in a little under the two hours predicted by David. He didn't park the car right outside but a short distance away so that it wouldn't be visible from inside the house.

'You tackle him on your own, in your own way. That's what I promised I'd let you do. I'll be generous and give you twenty minutes. Then I'm coming in. You have been warned.'

David kissed her, running his fingers slowly down her cheek and along the line of her chin.

'I love you,' he said. 'Now go and do what you have to do.'

Dr Marshall opened the door and was more than a little surprised to find Kate standing there.

'There's nothing the matter, is there, Kate?' he asked in an anxious voice.

'No, nothing at all,' said Kate, stepping inside. 'Are you alone?'

'What?'

'I mean is Nurse Hoyle here?'

'No, you've just missed her, as a matter of fact.'

Kate followed her father into the kitchen and they both sat down at the table.

'I came back today, Dad, because there's something I want to talk to you about. Something that I need to say face to face. Something I can't tell you over the phone.'

'It's not about David Firth, is it, by any chance?'

Her father's intuition caught Kate by surprise. For a moment she sat, silently staring down at the wooden table, unable to find the words she was looking for.

'Because if it is,' said Dr Marshall, 'I have something I must tell you. Ever since we had our conversation about him before my collapse, it triggered off some rather worrying thoughts in my own mind. Then yesterday, before you left, you mentioned him again. All evening, when I was on my own, I couldn't get him out of my mind. I began to think back to those...painful years. The years with Julia.

'At the time I tried to keep my unhappiness from you because you were so young and impressionable. But your stepmother was a very difficult woman to live with. I didn't want a divorce while you were still young, but by the time you were older, a teenager, I just couldn't stand life with her any more.

'It wasn't just her tantrums and hysterics. She was a sly, deceitful woman. I found out years later she had been having countless affairs. Everyone else knew about it, apparently. Everyone except me. You can imagine how that made me feel.

'What you said yesterday—about the possibility of Julia pestering David, trying to seduce him, instead of the other way round—made me think hard and deep. And the more I thought about it, the more I came to realise the truth of the matter. I'm now convinced that Julia was the one who was telling lies and deceiving me, not David Firth.'

Dr Marshall paused and got himself a drink of water from the tap. His hands were shaking as he put it down on the table.

'Oh, Dad,' said Kate, 'don't let it upset you. Everything's going to be all right.'

'That's just it,' said her father emotionally. 'It worries me very much that I was to blame for sending that young man packing. He was a brilliant student and would have made a wonderful doctor, yet I was responsible for ending his medical career. I shall feel guilty about it for the rest of my life because I will never know what happened to him.'

At that moment, as if on cue, the doorbell rang. Kate leapt up, knowing just who would be standing outside.

'I'll get it, Dad.'

She opened the door and a broad smile lit up her face as she saw David standing there. 'Come inside,' she said, 'It's going to be OK. Just don't say anything for a moment. Let me do the talking.'

'Who is it, Kate?' her father called from the kitchen.

'Someone I'd like you to meet,' she said, leading the way for David to follow.

As they entered the kitchen together, Dr Marshall looked puzzled. It was evident he didn't recognise David after twelve years, and in any event David was the last person he would have expected to walk into his house.

'Dad,' said Kate, 'this is one of my colleagues from the medical practice in the Lakes.'

Dr Marshall's face changed from puzzlement to comprehension. 'Oh, yes, of course,' he said. 'How nice to meet you. Doctor...?'

'David Firth,' said David, offering his hand in greeting. 'Dr David Firth.'

Now it was Dr Marshall's turn to be speechless.

'That's what I was trying to tell you, Dad. I met up with David when I joined the practice as a locum. I never seemed to be able to pick the right moment to give you the news, that's all.'

Dr Marshall's face registered surprise, relief and joy all at once.

'Dear boy,' he said, grasping David by the hand. 'I can't tell you how happy this makes me. To know that you finally made it through to being a doctor after all that...well, shall we say misunderstanding all those years ago.'

Dr Marshall stood back and looked at David and Kate, standing side by side.

'But why on earth have you come down here, David?' he asked, trying to weigh up the situation. 'Surely you haven't come to take revenge on me after all these years?' A wicked smile crossed his face. 'You wouldn't hit an old man with a bandage round his head, now, would you?'

David looked at him sternly. Then a warm smile spread across his face.

'I plan to take my revenge in a different sort of way, Dr Marshall. I'm going to steal something from you. Something very precious.

'Dr Marshall, I've come to ask for your daughter's hand in marriage.'

MEDICAL ROMANCE

WINNING HER BACK by Lilian Darcy

Medicine and marriage, Southshore has it all

Dr Grace Gaines was devastated by the loss of her baby, more so as it became clear that her husband Marcus had not wanted the child. Their marriage under threat, Marcus had taken a six month break, and now he was back. Would they stay married or not...

RULES OF ENGAGEMENT by Jean Evans

After her Uncle Jon suffers a heart attack, newly qualified doctor Jamie agrees to act as a locum at his general practice. Jon's partner, Dr Sam Paige, is not convinced she's up to the job. Her first priority is to prove herself and then make him realise she's a woman too! But is she too late...

FALLING FOR A STRANGER by Janet Ferguson

For ward sister Anna Chancellor, returning to work after what should have been her honeymoon was very hard. Being jilted made her feel she couldn't trust love again. Orthopaedic Registrar Daniel Mackay's disastrous marriage made him feel the same way. Can they dispense with caution and accept the love they've found?

Available from 2nd June 2000

Available at most branches of WH Smith, Tesco, Martins, Borders, Easons, Volume One/James Thin and most good paperback bookshops

0005/03a